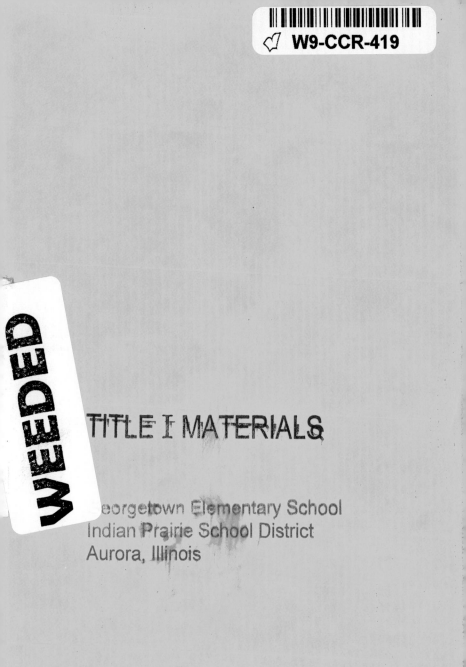

TITLE I MATERIALS

Georgetown Elementary School
Indian Prairie School District
Aurora, Illinois

SARAH WEEKS

Scholastic Press • New York

Library of Congress Cataloging-in-Publication Data

Weeks, Sarah.
Oggie Cooder / Sarah Weeks. — 1st ed.
p. cm.
Summary: Quirky fourth-grader Oggie Cooder goes from being
shunned to everyone's best friend when his uncanny ability to
chew slices of cheese into the shapes of states wins him a slot
on a popular television talent show, but he soon learns the perils
of being a celebrity — and having a neighbor girl as his manager.
ISBN-13: 978-0-439-92791-8 (hardcover : alk. paper)
ISBN-10: 0-439-92791-9 (hardcover : alk. paper)
[1. Eccentrics and eccentricities—Fiction. 2. Celebrities—
Fiction. 3. Ability—Fiction. 4. Self-esteem—Fiction.
5. Friendship—Fiction. 6. Schools—Fiction.] I. Title.
PZ7.W422150gg 2008
[Fic]—dc22

2007018645

ISBN-10: 0-439-92791-9
ISBN-13: 978-0-439-92791-8

10 9 8 7 6 5 4 3 2 1   08 09 10 11 12

Printed in the U.S.A.   23
First edition, February 2008

The text type was set in Janson Text
Book design by Elizabeth B. Parisi

for my friend, colleague,
and editor, David levithan

Oggie Cooder lay on the deserted sandy white beach sunbathing in a green and purple polka-dotted bathing suit he'd never seen before in his life. In his hand, he held a giant coconut filled with the most delicious drink he'd ever tasted, and all around him graceful palm trees swayed to and fro, dancing a hula to the sound of a distant ukulele. A fiery sun hung like a spitty yellow tennis ball overhead. Feeling the need to cool off, Oggie rose in his unfamiliar polka-dotted bathing suit, ran down to the water's edge, and waded in. As he paddled out into the crystal blue sea, the warm salty waves lapped against his cheek and the air was filled with the sweet tropical aroma of dog breath.

Wait a second, thought Oggie, *DOG BREATH?*

He opened his eyes. His dog, Turk, was standing next to him, licking his face. The whole thing had been a *dream*. Oggie wiped the dog slobber off his cheek and looked over at the clock. 7:45 on the dot.

"Good dog," he said, reaching over to give Turk a pat on the head. "You're a regular alarm clock. Except that you're furry. And you have fleas. And really bad breath."

Turk, whose real name was Turkey-On-Rye because that was the name of Oggie's favorite sandwich, barked and raced out of the room, only to return a minute later with a soggy yellow tennis ball in his mouth. He whined and wagged his giant tail, nearly knocking a lamp off the bedside table.

"Okay, okay, I get the message," said Oggie, sitting up and rubbing the sleep from his eyes. "Go get your leash and I'll walk you around the block before school."

And that was how Oggie Cooder, future famous cheese charving champion of the world, started his day.

*   *   *

By the time Oggie got back from walking Turk that morning, his parents had already left for work. They'd gone in early to meet with a plumber about fixing a leaky pipe that had been giving them some trouble at their store. Oggie poured himself a quick bowl of cereal and picked up the mail, which was sitting in a pile on the kitchen table.

"Bills, bills, junk, bills . . ." he said as he sorted through the letters. "Hold on. Is this what I think it is? *Yes!*" He held the long pale blue envelope aloft.

"*Prrrrr-ip! Prrrrr-ip!*" Oggie fluttered his tongue against the roof of his mouth. He always made that sound when he was excited about something. At the moment, the something he was excited about was a letter from the Bakestuff Company about the name-the-new-bagel contest he had entered several weeks earlier. Oggie loved contests, and had been waiting eagerly to hear whether he had won the grand prize — a trip to Hawaii. He'd been dreaming about sandy beaches and palm trees practically every night. Although he had never won anything in his life, he was hopeful that he might actually have a shot at winning the Bakestuff contest. Oggie was very proud of the name he had come up with for a cinnamon-raisin bagel. He had gotten the idea from something he'd overheard his mother say on the phone one day when she was talking to his Aunt Hettie.

"You better warn the neighbors ahead of time, Het, 'cause we're definitely going to be raisin' the roof," she'd said.

"What's the matter with Aunt Hettie's roof?" Oggie had asked his mother after she'd hung up.

Mrs. Cooder laughed.

"That's just an expression, Ogg," she explained. "'Raisin' the roof' means 'having a good time.' Your Aunt Hettie and I were talking about the family reunion we're going to have this summer."

"Is Uncle Vern coming?" Oggie asked hopefully.

Uncle Vern was Oggie's favorite relative. He drove a pickup truck with a jacked-up rear end, and he could make his belly button talk without using his hands.

"Yes, Uncle Vern will be there," Oggie's mother replied. "Which is probably something else I'd better remind Aunt Hettie to warn the neighbors about."

Uncle Vern and his talking belly button were far from Oggie's thoughts now as he ripped open the letter from the Bakestuff Company. "Raisin' the Roof is a perfect name for a cinnamon-raisin bagel, don't you think, Turk?" Oggie asked.

Turk wasn't paying attention. He was too busy sniffing around under the table looking for something to eat.

Oggie unfolded the letter and began to read.

Dear Mr. Cooder:
We thank you for your entry. However, we regret to inform you . . .

"Frappuccino!" cried Oggie in disappointment.

There was no cussing allowed in Oggie's house. Mrs. Cooder kept a big jar on the kitchen counter, and anyone who slipped up had to put a quarter in

it. Oggie didn't see the point of wasting his allowance on expensive cuss words when there were plenty of perfectly good free words you could use instead.

"Frappuccino. Frappuccino. Frappuccino . . ." Oggie grumbled as he read the rest of the letter.

Not only had the people at Bakestuff been unimpressed with the name he'd come up with for their new bagel, Oggie couldn't believe what they'd chosen instead.

"*Sunshine?* What kind of a name is that for a bagel?" he asked Turk. "It doesn't even have the word 'raisin' in it!"

Oggie crumpled the letter into a ball and threw it across the room, missing the wastebasket he'd been aiming for by a good foot and a half. Turk, who was always hungry, trotted over and wolfed down the balled-up letter in a couple of quick bites.

"I guess the only way I'm ever going to get to Hawaii is in my dreams," said Oggie sadly. He shoved his homework and his lunch into his backpack. Then, as he was about to walk out the door, he suddenly remembered something. He went to the fridge, got out two slices of processed American cheese, and slipped them into his back pocket.

That cheese would change Oggie Cooder's life forever. Because while sometimes the road to fame and fortune is paved in gold, there are other times when it's made of cheese. Processed American cheese, to be exact.

2

Directly across the street from the Cooders' house, Donnica Perfecto was sitting at the breakfast table doing what she did best — whining.

"You don't really expect me to eat this toast, do you?" she asked her mother. "It's *burnt*."

"I'm sorry, Cupcake," said Mrs. Perfecto. "I'm not used to that new toaster yet."

"It's top of the line, Miriam, nothing wrong with that toaster," Mr. Perfecto piped up from behind his newspaper. "They really turned up the dial with this one. Took toasty and made it toastier. Most people would kill to have that kind of firepower on the counter."

"Yes, dear. It's just that with the old one, the toast popped up when it was done," said Mrs. Perfecto.

"Popping up is old-fashioned, Miriam," Mr. Perfecto insisted.

Mrs. Perfecto sighed. "If you say so, dear."

"Daddy?" said Donnica, poking absentmindedly at her toast with a pink-glitter-polished fingertip. "This year for my birthday, can we buy a house in Hollywood and move there?"

"*Hollywood?*" cried Mr. and Mrs. Perfecto at the same time.

From the moment she could talk, if you asked Donnica Perfecto what she wanted to be when she grew up, she would say the same thing — "Famous!" Her parents had shelled out a considerable amount of money over the years for music, dance, and acting lessons, but it had become painfully clear that Donnica had absolutely no talent in any of those arenas. Even so, she was sure she was going to become a star.

"Why would we want to move to Hollywood?" asked Mr. Perfecto.

"Well, you don't really expect me to live *here* forever, do you?" whined Donnica.

"What's wrong with Wawatosa?" Mrs. Perfecto wondered.

"It's in *Wisconsin*," Donnica said disgustedly, flicking her burnt toast with a finger and scattering a sooty shower of black crumbs across the clean white tablecloth. "How am I supposed to get discovered in a place where the only thing that's famous is *cheese*?"

George Perfecto owned a large discount appliance store out on Stadium Boulevard called Big Dealz. The license plates on the two silver SUVs in the Perfectos' driveway said BIG ONE and BIG TWO. Donnica's room was painted her favorite color, bubble gum pink. She had her own private bathroom and a closet full of expensive clothes, a queen-size canopy bed, and a minifridge stocked with her favorite drink, imported apricot fruit water — which, if you read the label carefully, was actually bottled in Hoboken, New Jersey.

Things were a little different over at the Cooders' house. Mr. and Mrs. Cooder had only one car, an old Volvo station wagon, which had definitely seen better days. They drank their water from the tap, and the whole family shared a single bathroom. With the exception of underwear and socks, which Mrs. Cooder purchased new from Selznick's department store, all of their clothes came from Too Good to Be Threw, the resale shop that the Cooders owned and ran in downtown Wawatosa.

Mrs. Cooder wore exclusively purple clothing, plum being her signature shade, and she was also very fond of unusual hats. Mr. Cooder favored bowling shirts with other people's names embroidered over the pockets. Oggie didn't care about clothes at all. His method of getting dressed in the morning was to yank a pair of pants out of the closet, pull a shirt out of the drawer, put them on whether or not they really went together, and be done with it.

If the pants in the closet and the shirts in the drawers had been ordinary things, like T-shirts and jeans, Oggie might have looked like any other fourth-grade boy who had gotten dressed in a hurry. But since it was Mrs. Cooder who chose the things that went into Oggie's closet and drawers, he sometimes ended up with crazy-looking outfits. On the day Oggie received the disappointing news from the Bakestuff Company, he was wearing blue-and-white-striped seersucker pants and a plaid duck-hunting shirt — complete with a pouch for carrying dead ducks, which, of course, he was *not* planning to do. On his feet, he wore size-11 sneakers, with laces he had crocheted out of colorful yarn.

It was during a visit to Zanesville, Ohio, that Oggie's Aunt Hettie had taught him how to crochet. She hadn't done it out of the goodness of her heart. She'd done it in order to keep him out of her garden. Oggie, who'd been only five years old at the time and bored to tears with listening to grown-up talk, had wandered out into the garden, where he decided to pretend he was on the moon.

He'd imagined that the garden was a big crater, and the birdbath was his rocket ship. Aunt Hettie, spying him out her window, had let it be known in no uncertain terms that she did not appreciate

Oggie moonwalking through her zucchini plants, and she did not appreciate him digging for moon rocks in her potato patch. She *especially* did not appreciate Oggie sitting in her birdbath with one of her good mixing bowls on his head shouting *Blast off!* and scaring all the birds away. So Oggie had explained that what *he* didn't appreciate was that the most exciting thing to do at Aunt Hettie's house was to eat a whole bunch of cucumbers for lunch and then sit around waiting for the burping to begin. Aunt Hettie had laughed and pulled a crochet hook out of her apron pocket.

"Come here, Oggie Cooder," she'd said, sitting down on the porch step and patting a spot beside her. So Oggie went and sat down beside his aunt and let her teach him how to crochet shoelaces. He'd been making them ever since. Some of the kids at school, the kind of kids who are always looking for a reason to be mean, made fun of him for doing it.

"Weirdo."

"Dork."

"Doofus."

"Dweeb."

Oggie couldn't help it that he liked to do things a little differently than other people did. He was who he was. And even though there were times when his oddness made life a little bit difficult, if Oggie Cooder had been anybody *other* than who he was, the extraordinary thing that was about to happen to him never would have occurred.

3

Oggie Cooder and Donnica Perfecto were both in Mr. Snolinovsky's class at Truman Elementary School. On the first day of school, Mr. Snolinovsky wrote his name on the board and made everybody practice saying it slowly a few times. SNOW-LINN-OFF-SKEE. Oggie had never had a man teacher before, although he had noticed that several of his previous teachers had very hairy arms.

In kindergarten, Oggie had been in Mrs. Foerster's class. He had liked Mrs. Foerster. She had pretty blue eyes, wore flowery perfume, and because she had been raised somewhere in the South, when she talked, she had a gooey way of stretching out her words that made it sound like she was saying something nice, even when she wasn't.

On his final report card that year, Mrs. Foerster had written: *Oggie is a very unusual child.* One example she gave of Oggie's unusualness was his tendency to grin when he was being scolded. When Oggie's mother asked him why he did that, he explained that it wasn't because he thought getting in trouble was a joke, it was just that when Mrs. Foerster got mad, sometimes she said funny things. For instance, the time she caught Oggie trying to sharpen a carrot — which he insisted he'd stuck into the electric sharpener by accident, thinking it was a No. 2 pencil — she said, "You can put your boots in the oven, Oggie Cooder, but that don't make 'em biscuits."

Some parents might not have been happy about the word *unusual* being used to describe their child, but Mr. and Mrs. Cooder were perfectly fine with it. They made their living collecting unusual things at garage sales and auctions and reselling them at Too Good to Be Threw. As far as they were concerned, the more unusual an object was, the more value it had.

Over the years, Oggie's teachers had found all kinds of interesting ways to describe him — *unique, quirky, one-of-a-kind.* Last year, in third grade, Oggie's teacher, Mrs. Stifler, had said that Oggie *marched to the beat of a different drummer.* Oggie had found that comment surprising, considering the only instrument he knew how to play was the kazoo, and Mrs. Stifler had specifically told him never to bring it to school again because it was a) incredibly annoying and b) extremely spitty. (Later, Oggie's father had explained to him that saying someone marches to the beat of a different drummer is just another way of saying that a person is unusual, unique, quirky, and one-of-a-kind. Then his mother had taken out the rubber cement and had carefully glued the report card into the family scrapbook alongside all the others.)

Oggie sometimes wondered what Mr. Snolinovsky was going to write about him on his fourth-grade report card. But this particular morning, he was too busy thinking about having lost the name-the-bagel contest to think about much else. As he made his way to school in his seersucker pants and duck-hunting shirt, he noticed Donnica Perfecto up ahead, her bubble-gum-pink backpack slung over one shoulder. She was walking with Hannah Hummerman and Dawn Perchy, two other girls from Oggie's class. Oggie had an idea.

"Hey, you guys!" he called out to them. "Wait up a sec!"

Donnica glanced over her shoulder at Oggie, then whispered something to the other girls. They all began to walk faster.

Oggie started running and finally caught up with them at the corner, where they'd gotten hung up waiting for the light to change.

"I guess you didn't hear me calling," Oggie panted. He was a little sweaty from his run, so he wiped his forehead with his sleeve.

"Ewww," said Donnica. "Guh —"

"— ross!" Hannah and Dawn said in unison, providing the ending of the word.

"What do you want, anyway?" Donnica asked.

"I was thinking, since it's Thursday, which means we've got a spelling test today, maybe we could all walk together and quiz each other on the words on the way."

"Puh —" said Hannah.

"Watch it," Donnica snapped. "*I* do the first syllables."

"Sorry," said Hannah, hanging her head.

"Puh —" said Donnica.

"— leeze!" added Hannah and Dawn together.

Satisfied, Donnica nodded and pulled a tube of cherry-flavored lip gloss out of her pocket. Immediately, the other two girls did the same thing, and all three of them got busy rubbing sticky pink goo onto their mouths.

"Nice outfit," said Donnica to Oggie, as she recapped the gloss and slipped it back into her pocket. "Let me guess — is that from your parents' store?"

"Yeppers," said Oggie as he smoothed the front of his shirt with his hand. He didn't notice Hannah poke Dawn in the ribs or how they were both biting their cheeks to keep from laughing. "So do you want to practice the spelling words?" he continued. "I even made some flash cards." He fished around in his duck pouch and pulled out a bunch of beat-up index cards riddled with what appeared to be tooth marks. "Turk tried to eat them, but don't worry, most of the spit should be dry by now."

Donnica sighed loudly and tucked a loose strand of long, honey-gold hair behind her ear.

"I've got two words for you, Oggie Cooder, and they're both *EEEEW.*"

When the light changed, Donnica Perfecto and her glossy-lipped posse stepped off the curb. As they flounced away, Donnica called back over her shoulder, "*Love* your shoelaces, Oggie Cooder!"

"Thanks!" said Oggie, completely missing the sarcastic tone in her voice. "I made them myself."

"Loo —" said Donnica under her breath.

"— zer!" added Dawn and Hannah, and the three of them dissolved in a fit of high-pitched giggling.

As Oggie watched them walk away, he sighed and reached for his back pocket — this would be such a perfect time to charve, he thought. But he stopped himself. He really should study his spelling flash cards once more before he got to school.

The charving would have to wait a little longer.

4

ater that morning at school, Oggie was sitting at his desk daydreaming about how great it would have been if he had won the Bakestuff name-the-bagel contest. He pictured himself strolling into the grocery store and running into one of his classmates. David Korben, for instance.

"Hey, Oggie," David would say. "You sure do have a nice tan."

"That's because I just got back from Hawaii," Oggie would tell him.

"Oh, that's right, I heard about how you won that contest."

Then David would pick up a bag of Raisin' the Roof bagels, which just happened to be on display nearby. "Are these the ones you named?" he'd ask.

Oggie would nod and smile modestly.

"That's pretty cool," David would say. "Hey, you don't happen to be free after school today to come over and shoot some hoops with me and the guys, do you?"

Oggie would have loved an invitation to play basketball with the guys, but it was about as likely to happen as Donnica Perfecto inviting him over to one of her pool parties. David Korben and his jock buddies had given Oggie the nickname Duck because in gym class, no matter what kind of ball you threw at him, Oggie always ducked. And as for Donnica's pool, Oggie had never even seen it, though he had heard kids splashing around in it plenty of times during the summer.

Oggie's seat was directly in front of the teacher's desk, so when Mr. Snolinovsky clapped his hands to announce that it was time for the spelling test, Oggie, who was still daydreaming, was so startled he jumped right out of his seat. Unfortunately, he missed it on the way back down and ended up on the floor in a heap. Bethie Hudson, who sat right behind Oggie, rolled her eyes.

"Remember, class," Mr. Snolinovsky said as Oggie picked himself up off the floor and slid back into his seat, "you are to use each spelling word in a sentence and the sentences must make sense."

He gave them ten minutes to complete the test.

The words they had been assigned that week ended in the letters *o-u-s*. Oggie knew how to spell them all, thanks to his handy dandy flash cards. When Mr. Snolinovsky told them it was time to put their pencils down, Oggie felt fairly confident that he'd done well on the test.

"We're going to try something new today," Mr. Snolinovsky announced. "Instead of marking your tests myself, I'm going to ask you to mark one another's work. Please pass your paper up one seat to the person sitting directly in front of you."

Bethie Hudson groaned and rolled her big blue eyes again. Oggie didn't hear her, though, he was too busy worrying about what to do with his paper.

"No offense, Mr. Snolinovsky, but I don't get it," Oggie said. "You told us that we were supposed to pass our papers to the person sitting in front of us, right? But how am I supposed to pass my paper to the person sitting in front of me when there isn't anybody sitting in front of me, except for you, and you're not even sitting there at the moment, you're standing over by the blackboard scratching your head?"

"Could you have possibly found a longer, more complicated way of asking that question, Oggie?" Mr. Snolinovsky laughed.

"I'm not sure," said Oggie, "but I'll give it a try if you want me to."

Mr. Snolinovsky had been kidding, but Oggie didn't get it. He often took things the wrong way. Either that or he was saying something he shouldn't — like the time he asked Mrs. Stifler if the reason her stomach was so big was because she was expecting triplets. Mrs. Stifler hadn't been too happy about that question, since she wasn't even expecting one baby at the time, let alone three.

"If, like Oggie, you happen to be sitting in the front row," Mr. Snolinovsky explained to the class, "I'd like you to get up and quietly take your paper to the person sitting in the last seat in your row."

There was a flurry of activity as people passed their papers. Oggie got up and carried his test back to America Johnson, who was the last person sitting in his row. America had a twin sister, Asia, who was in the other fourth-grade class at Truman. Oggie sometimes wondered whether Mr. and Mrs. Johnson were planning to have any more kids and, if so, whether they'd be naming them after continents, too. He thought Antarctica Johnson had a nice ring to it.

"You get to do mine," Oggie said, handing his paper to America.

"Lucky me," said America flatly.

When he returned to his seat, Bethie's spelling test was sitting on Oggie's desk.

"The first word is *ridiculous*," Mr. Snolinovsky began. He slowly spelled the word for them: "R-i-d-i-c-u-l-o-u-s."

Oggie didn't even have to look at Bethie's paper to know that she had spelled the word right. Bethie Hudson had great big front teeth that reminded Oggie of piano keys, and she was the best speller in the class.

"Please make sure that the word is spelled correctly and that it has been used properly in a sentence," Mr. Snolinovsky said. "If the person whose paper you are marking has successfully accomplished both of those things, you may place a check mark next to the answer."

Bethie had written: *Ridiculous is a ridiculously easy word to spell.*

Oggie put a big check mark next to Bethie's answer.

Mr. Snolinovsky cleared his throat, ready to move on to the next word, when he noticed that America's hand was raised.

"Question?" said Mr. Snolinovsky.

"What do we do if the person spelled the word right, but the sentence doesn't make any sense?" America asked.

Good question, thought Oggie, until it occurred to him that the sentence America was talking about was *his*.

Oggie suddenly felt nervous. He reached for his back pocket, knowing that a little charving would calm him down. The only problem was, Mr.

Snolinovsky had a strict rule against food in the classroom. Oggie took his hand out of his pocket and sighed. It looked like he was going to have to face this difficult moment without any help from his cheese.

5

r. Snolinovsky asked America to read Oggie's sentence out loud.

"It says, 'Someone is a ridiculous man funny bongo,'" said America.

Everybody laughed.

"That's not what is says," said Oggie. "You read it wrong."

"No, I didn't," said America defensively. "That's what you wrote. 'Someone is a ridiculous man funny bongo.'"

More laughter.

"That doesn't even make sense," said Oggie.

"See?" said America. "He agrees it doesn't make sense, and he wrote it!"

The whole class was really enjoying this. David Korben laughed so hard, he actually snorted.

"Calm down, everybody," said Mr. Snolinovsky. "America, please bring me Oggie's paper."

America, holding Oggie's spelling test by the corner, carried it up to Mr. Snolinovsky, who looked at it for a minute, then scratched his head.

"I'm sorry, Oggie," he said, "but I'm having a little difficulty reading your handwriting myself. I'd like to hear what you wrote. Would you mind reading it for us?"

He handed the test paper to Oggie, who smoothed it out on his desk and slowly ran his finger along under the words as he read: "'Sunshine is a ridiculous name for a bagel.'"

"That doesn't make any more sense than the bongo one," snorted Donnica. She pulled out her lip gloss to apply a fresh coat, instantly causing Dawn and Hannah to do the same thing.

"What do you mean?" said Oggie. "It does so make sense."

"You're cuckoo in the coconut, Cooder," said Jackson Polito, crossing his eyes and twirling a finger around next to his ear.

"If he calls his bagel Sunshine, what do you think he calls his hamburger? Sweetheart?" David shouted out.

Some kids were hooting and clapping by now.

"Quiet down, please," said Mr. Snolinovsky. "Let's give Oggie a chance to explain."

Oggie was grateful for the opportunity.

"Sunshine wasn't my idea," he began. "My idea was Raisin' the Roof, because of the raisins."

"Aww, isn't that nice, he's building a little house for his raisins," said Jackson.

"No, I'm not," insisted Oggie. "Raisin' the roof means having fun, and I figured Bakestuff probably wanted people to think eating their bagels would be fun, right?"

"I'm not sure I'm following," said Mr. Snolinovsky, scratching his head again. "Why exactly is the bagel named Sunshine?"

"Beats me," said Oggie, shrugging his shoulders and shaking his head. "If you ask me, Raisin' the Roof is a much better name."

To the amusement of Oggie's classmates, it was soon revealed that the rest of his spelling sentences were also about bagels:

It was a VICIOUS idea to name the bagel Sunshine.

There is nothing DELICIOUS about a bagel named Sunshine.

It would have been more GENEROUS to name the bagel Raisin' the Roof.

It took a while, but Oggie finally managed to explain about the contest he had entered. Mr. Snolinovsky agreed that under the circumstances, Oggie's sentences, though unusual, did in fact make sense. Not all of the kids agreed.

"Weirdo."

"Dork."

"Doofus."

"Dweeb."

Oggie slipped his hand into his back pocket again and touched the cheese. Boy, did he ever feel like charving now. Donnica Perfecto frowned at him and turned up her pointy little nose. Little did she know that it would only be a matter of time before Oggie Cooder would be holding her ticket to Hollywood in the very same hand that was touching that slice of American cheese.

b

At lunch, Oggie sat at his usual table in the corner next to the garbage cans. The only other person sitting there was Amy Schneider. Oggie and Amy sat together every day at lunch, but it wasn't because they were friends. The way it worked at Truman was that every lunch table had a crowd of kids who sat together because of something they had in common. There was the jock table where David Korben and his basketball buddies sat, and there was the table for girls who liked horses where Bethie Hudson and all her horsey little girlfriends sat. Donnica Perfecto had dibs on a choice table by the window, where she and Hannah and Dawn ate lunch together every day.

There were lots of tables in the cafeteria, but not one of them was for people like Oggie who liked to crochet shoelaces and charve cheese. Charving cheese was one of Oggie's favorite hobbies and, in a sense, Amy Schneider had been the one who'd discovered it.

The Schneiders had moved to town right after the school year began, and Amy was placed in Mr. Snolinovsky's class. On her first day at Truman, when nobody made any attempt to be friendly or invite her to sit at their lunch tables, Amy noticed there were empty seats at Oggie's table. She asked him if it would be okay if she sat there, too.

"Sure," said Oggie, who happened to be eating a piece of cheese at the time.

Amy was painfully shy. Plus, she had a mouth full of metal braces, with a complicated crisscrossing of colored rubber bands connecting her top teeth to the bottom ones in a way that made it difficult for her to open her mouth. She took the rubber bands off to eat, but the rest of the time she had to keep them on. Between her shyness and the rubber bands, she hardly ever talked, and when she did, it was usually in a whisper. Oggie tried asking her a couple of questions that first day to be polite, but it was so noisy in the cafeteria he couldn't hear her answers. Finally, he gave up and went back to eating his cheese.

He was sitting there, absentmindedly nibbling away, when suddenly Amy whispered —

"*Florida.*"

"What?" Oggie asked, wondering why this strange new girl was talking about Florida all of a sudden.

Amy pointed at the cheese in his hand.

"It's Florida," she said.

Sure enough, without meaning to, somehow Oggie had managed to bite his cheese into the shape of the state of Florida.

When he got home from school that day, he took an economy pack of cheese slices out of the refrigerator, got the big atlas off the shelf, and spent several hours practicing charving the cheese into the shape of all fifty states.

Charving, a word he made up by combining the words *chewing* and *carving*, was something Oggie discovered he not only enjoyed, but also found very relaxing. That's why, after the nerve-racking experience of having to defend his bagel-related spelling sentences in front of the whole class, Oggie felt that a little charving was exactly what he needed. Sitting there in the lunchroom across the table from Amy Schneider, he was relieved to finally be able to pull out one of the slices of cheese he'd been carrying in his back pocket all day and get down to business.

The reason Oggie didn't keep the cheese in his lunch bag or his backpack was that he had discovered his back pocket was the only place that could be depended upon to keep the cheese at exactly the right temperature for charving. If the cheese got too cold, it would crack, and if it was too warm, it became sticky and hard to handle.

Oggie decided to charve Texas. Some states were easier than others. For instance, Kansas, which was basically a square piece of cheese with the upper right-hand corner chewed off, was about as easy as it got. Texas happened to be one of the most challenging. Oggie had just nibbled down the western side of the state and was heading east toward the panhandle when he suddenly burped, causing him to take too large a bite and ruin the whole thing.

"*Frappuccino*," he said, tossing the mangled cheese down on the table.

Without a word, Amy opened her sandwich and pulled out a limp, mayonnaise-coated piece of white cheese, offering it across the table to Oggie.

"No, thanks," he told her. "Swiss cheese is no good for charving. Too many holes. Don't worry, though, I have an extra piece of good old American right here," he said, patting his back pocket. "I always carry two."

Amy shrugged and stuck the cheese back in her sandwich, while Oggie pulled the straw off the back of his juice box and stabbed it into the fruit punch a little too hard, causing a stream of red liquid to squirt out and hit him in the face. He stuck out his tongue just in time to catch a drop of juice as it slid off his chin.

Amy covered her mouth and giggled, then handed Oggie the napkin out of her lunch box.

Maybe the road to fame and fortune was not the only path that would turn out to be paved with cheese.

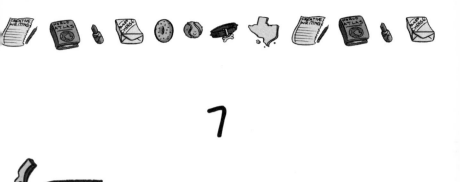

7

After lunch, Mr. Snolinovsky's class always did science and math. Then they would finish the day with an hour of creative writing.

Creative writing was Oggie's worst subject. For one thing, his handwriting was horrible — which was one of the reasons America hadn't been able to read his spelling sentence earlier in the day. But the bigger problem was that Oggie could never seem to think of anything he wanted to write about.

"Ideas are like seeds," Mr. Snolinovsky had explained to the class one day. "Plant a seed and you'll grow a story."

Oggie had stayed after school that day to ask Mr. Snolinovsky a question.

43

"Where do those story seeds you were talking about come from?"

Mr. Snolinovsky tapped the side of his head. "In here," he said. "And here, too." He tapped the left side of his chest, over his heart. "We're all full of seeds, Oggie."

"You mean like all watermelons are full of seeds?" Oggie asked.

Mr. Snolinovsky smiled and said, "Yes. Exactly."

"That's what I was afraid of," sighed Oggie.

"What do you mean?" Mr. Snolinovsky asked.

"My Aunt Hettie has a garden and she grows watermelons that look like regular watermelons from the outside, but when you cut them open they don't have any seeds in them at all."

Mr. Snolinovsky scratched his head.

"I think I know what you're trying to say," he told Oggie, "but believe me when I tell you that you're a very interesting person, Oggie Cooder. And unlike your aunt's watermelons, interesting people always have seeds in them."

Oggie liked that Mr. Snolinovsky had chosen the words "very interesting" to describe him, but he was not convinced that what his teacher had said about the seeds was true. As he sat at his desk listening to the *scritch-scratch* of pencils going on all around him, Oggie's mind was a total blank. Not a seed in sight. Finally, he raised his hand.

"May I go get a drink of water?" he asked.

Mr. Snolinovsky nodded, and Oggie went out into the hall to the drinking fountain. He took several long gulps of cool water, and when he lifted his head to wipe his mouth, he looked down the hall and noticed a very short man standing outside the school office with a cardboard box in his arms. The man was bald and had dark sunglasses pushed up onto his forehead. As Oggie watched, the man placed the box on the floor, opened it up, and took out a piece of bright pink paper. Then, standing on the box in order to help him reach, he tacked the pink paper up on the school bulletin board. The man noticed Oggie watching him.

"Check it out," he called down the hall to Oggie. "You never know, kid. This could be your big break."

Oggie wasn't sure what the man was talking about. But even though he was curious, he was afraid if he took the time to walk down the hall to look at the bulletin board, Mr. Snolinovsky might notice he was taking too long to get his drink. He didn't want to get in trouble.

"Three o'clock tomorrow afternoon at the Bandshell," the man called, then jumped down off the box, picked it up, and left. Oggie went back to his classroom, telling himself to be sure to remember to stop and look at the pink flyer after school to find out what it was all about.

As he opened the door, he ran right smack into Donnica Perfecto, who was on her way out of the classroom with a bathroom pass in her hand.

"Excuse *you*," said Donnica as she pushed past him.

* * *

Oggie had hoped that taking a water break might somehow loosen his brain enough to make a story seed fall out of it. But nothing like that seemed to be happening. Mr. Snolinovsky noticed that Oggie was having trouble and came over to talk to him.

"Can I ask you something, Oggie?"

"Sure."

"Do you have any pets?"

"Yeppers. A dog named Turk. He's the best."

"Does he ever do funny things?"

"Sure," said Oggie.

"Like what?" Mr. Snolinovsky asked.

"Like this one time he buried a bone under my mother's pillow and another time he found a bag of black licorice and —"

Mr. Snolinovsky held up his hand to stop Oggie.

"Write it, Oggie," he said.

Oggie was confused. "Write what?" he asked.

"The story about what Turk did with the black licorice," Mr. Snolinovsky told him. "That's a seed."

"It is?" said Oggie, lighting up.

When the final bell rang, Oggie had already used up two pages (front and back) writing his story, and he hadn't even gotten to the part about Turk throwing up yet.

He put his story in his backpack in case he wanted to work on it some more at home. Then he got his jacket out of the closet, waved good-bye to Mr. Snolinovksy, and started down the hall. As he walked past the bulletin board, he suddenly remembered the man he'd seen earlier and stopped to take a look at the pink flyer. Only it wasn't there. Oggie searched the whole board twice, but there wasn't anything even remotely pink and there wasn't anything that mentioned an event taking place at the Bandshell on Friday, either.

"Weird," said Oggie.

"You sure are," someone said right behind him.

Oggie turned around in time to see David Korben disappearing around the corner with a basketball tucked under his arm.

*   *   *

Oggie stopped at the library before heading home that afternoon. Otherwise, he might have run into Donnica Perfecto and her posse as they stood on the corner waiting for the light to change.

"You guys are coming over to my house now, right?" Dawn said.

A sudden gust of wind whipped Donnica's hair across her face. She quickly brushed it away and then put her hand in her pocket. She felt the pink paper flyer there and pushed it down deeper. She didn't want anyone to see it, especially not Dawn or Hannah.

"I can't come over today," Donnica said.

"Why not?" asked Hannah.

"I've got a stomachache." Donnica suddenly grabbed her middle and grimaced as if she were in horrible pain. "Actually, I think my appendix might be exploding."

"Are you okay?" both girls asked, full of concern.

"I'll be fine," Donnica replied. "But I think I better go straight home, just in case I need to go to the hospital, or anything."

"That's strange," said Dawn as Donnica hurried away, still clutching her stomach. "She seemed perfectly fine a minute ago, didn't she?"

As it turned out, Dawn and Hannah were right to be suspicious. Donnica Perfecto was definitely up to something. The question was . . . *what*?

8

When Oggie walked in the door, Turk went crazy as usual, barking and wagging his tail so hard he actually fell over. Oggie got down on his knees and gave Turk's belly a nice scratch, which set the big dog's tail thumping happily against the floor like a tom-tom.

"Did you miss me, Turkey Boy?" he said. "How about we brush you this afternoon? Would you like that?" Turk's tail was wagging so fast now, it looked like it might come right off.

The phone rang. It was Mrs. Cooder calling from the store.

"I need you to come help this afternoon," she told Oggie. "Wouldn't you know we'd spring a leak right in the middle of inventory? The plumbers had to tear down the whole back wall this morning. It's a mess in here."

"I was just about to brush Turk," Oggie told his mother.

"Well, when you're finished, hop on your bike and come down, okay, Ogg? I'll order us a pizza."

"*Prrrrr-ip! Prrrrr-ip!*" said Oggie, whose absolute favorite food was pizza.

"What do you want on it?" asked his mother. "The usual?"

"Yeppers!" Oggie said happily.

Across the street, Donnica flopped down on her bed and took a big bite of one of the vanilla-frosted oatmeal cookies her mother had set out for her after-school snack. She reached over and flipped open the minifridge, pulling a bottle of apricot fruit water off the shelf and unscrewing the plastic cap with her teeth. Then she reached into her pocket and pulled out the pink flyer she'd torn off the school bulletin board when she'd noticed it on her way to the bathroom.

Callin' all kids.

Hidden Talents
is coming to your town!

We're combing the country in search of kids who can do something cool that nobody else can do. Come show our panel of judges what you've got. The quirkier, the better!

Auditions at The Wawatosa Bandshell. Friday, 3:00 pm sharp!

Donnica still couldn't believe it. *Hidden Talents* was one of the most popular shows on TV. She hadn't missed a single episode of the first season, staying glued to the television set until finally a fourteen-year-old boy from Nebraska beat out the competition to win the grand prize by playing "The Star-Spangled Banner" with a wet hand in his armpit. Donnica was certain that if she could land a spot on the show, it would be the big break she'd been waiting for her whole life. There was only one problem.

"MOM!" Donnica called at the top of her lungs.

"I'm downstairs, Cupcake!" her mother called back.

"Obviously!" Donnica yelled. "But I'm upstairs, so come up here. I need to ask you something."

Mrs. Perfecto arrived a minute later, flushed from her climb and carrying the bag of oatmeal cookies.

"What is it, dear? Do you want more cookies?"

"No, I want you to help me figure out what hidden talent I have."

Mrs. Perfecto put her index finger to her chin and thought for a moment.

"Hmmmm," she said. "Hidden talent? Well, you do have a very loud voice. But I wouldn't say you keep that talent *hidden* exactly."

"Having a loud voice isn't a talent, Mother," Donnica said with a pout.

"What about white teeth? Does that count?" asked Mrs. Perfecto. "You have very white teeth. Which reminds me, I need to make an appointment for you to have your regular checkup with Dr. Schelkun."

"Mom," Donnica said impatiently, "can you please stop talking about teeth and help me think of something quirky that I can do that nobody else can?"

Mrs. Perfecto tried her best, but she couldn't think of a thing.

"There must be *something*," Donnica insisted. "Everybody's good at *something*, right?"

"True," said Mrs. Perfecto. "Your friend Hannah is very good at ballet, and when Dawn plays that flute of hers, she sounds good enough to be in a professional orchestra."

Donnica was well aware of Hannah's dancing abilities and Dawn's musical skills. Their talents, not to mention the talents of various other kids she knew at Truman, were the reason she'd ripped the pink flyer down in the first place. Undoubtedly, other flyers had been put up around town, but she figured anything she could do to keep the competition down was worth it.

"We're not talking about Dawn and Hannah right now, Mother," snapped Donnica. "We're talking about *me.*"

"Of course we are, Cupcake. And I'm sure you're filled to the brim with talent, too. It's just that in your case it's extremely well hidden, that's all."

After Mrs. Perfecto left, Donnica rolled over and lay on her back on her bubble-gum-pink bedspread, staring up at the ceiling. She had to think of something, *anything* she could do to impress the judges from *Hidden Talents.* She heard a dog barking outside and turned her head toward the window just in time to catch sight of Oggie Cooder sitting on his porch brushing his dog. The air was filled with floating hair balls.

"Ugh," she said, wrinkling her pointy little nose in disgust.

When Oggie finished brushing Turk, he pulled something square and orange out of his pocket. At first Donnica thought it was a wallet, but when he put it in his mouth, she realized it was a piece of cheese.

Why is he eating it that way? wondered Donnica, pushing herself up onto her elbows in order to get a clearer view.

A minute later, Oggie let out a whoop of joy and waved his masterpiece in the air.

"*Prrrrr-ip! Prrrrr-ip!* Check it out, Turk! My best ever!"

Donnica's mouth fell open. Even from across the street she could recognize the shape Oggie had nibbled his cheese into.

"Texas," she said in amazement.

Suddenly, a lightbulb went on over her head. She jumped off the bed and ran to the window. Yanking

it open, she shouted down, "Oggie Cooder, don't you move!" Then she turned and raced out of her room, flying down the stairs, past her surprised mother, out the front door, and across the street to the Cooders' house.

When she would think back on this moment later, Donnica Perfecto would regret two things: one, that she had left the pink flyer lying on her bed, and two, that in her haste, she had neglected to close the window.

9

ggie was very surprised when Donnica yelled out the window at him, but not as surprised as Turk was. Even though Oggie had tied the end of the leash around the banister, Turk got so excited when he heard Donnica yelling that he pulled it loose. As soon as he realized he was free, Turk took off on a tear.

"Hey!" yelled Oggie. "Come back here!"

By the time Donnica arrived, Turk was already out of sight.

"I need . . . to talk . . . to you . . . about that . . . cheese," she panted.

"I can't talk right now," Oggie told her. "I have to catch my dog."

Turk shot out from between two houses, a

garden hose clamped between his teeth. When the hose reached the limit of its length, it jerked tight with a loud *BOING!*, sending Turk flying backward into a muddy flower bed. Oggie made a dive for his dog, but Turk was too fast for him.

"Turk! Sit!" Oggie shouted.

Turk immediately sat down and began scooching his backside along the sidewalk — something Mrs. Cooder often scolded him for doing on the hall carpet.

"Guh —" said Donnica, momentarily forgetting that nobody was around to supply the ends of her words.

When Turk made a pit stop at a fire hydrant, Oggie made another attempt to snag him. But again Turk was too quick.

"He's headed for your house!" Oggie yelled over his shoulder to Donnica. "Come on!"

Donnica joined in the chase as Turk went careening around the Perfectos' neatly manicured lawn, knocking over several clay flowerpots and then jumping the fence in a very ungraceful manner.

SPLASH!

Oggie stopped running and looked at Donnica. "Uh-oh," he said.

Oggie had never seen the Perfectos' pool, but he knew it was on the other side of that fence. As Oggie cooled himself off by running through the sprinkler in his front yard on hot summer days, Hannah and Dawn would ride by on their bikes wearing swimsuits and flip-flops. Donnica would open the gate for them and soon their happy shrieks and the smell of hot dogs grilling would waft over the fence, making both Oggie and Turk raise their noses in the air and sniff longingly.

Sure enough, when Donnica pushed open the gate this time, there was Turk, paddling around in the Perfectos' kidney-shaped pool, leaving a trail of grass and mud behind him as he went.

Mrs. Perfecto came running out onto the patio. "What in the world?" she cried. "Who let that disgusting creature in the pool?"

"Sorry, Mrs. Perfecto," said Oggie. "That's my dog, Turk."

"What on earth is he doing in the pool?"

Oggie was about to launch into the whole story, when Donnica jumped in.

"It's not Oggie's fault," she said. "I told him to put his dog in the pool. I wanted to see if he could swim."

Oggie was surprised. Why was Donnica lying to her mother? He was perfectly willing to take the blame for Turk. But before he could say anything, Mrs. Perfecto turned on her heel and started back into the house.

"If it makes you happy, Cupcake, that's all that matters," she called over her shoulder. "There are clean towels in the cabana banana if you need them."

"Cabana banana?" Oggie asked. It sounded even more ridiculous than a bagel named Sunshine.

"She means that thing," Donnica explained, pointing to a long, yellow plastic storage chest sitting next to the pool. "That's where we keep the towels for when we have guests."

"Oh," said Oggie, who, of course, had never been a guest at one of the Perfectos' pool parties.

"You know, Oggie," said Donnica sweetly, "you really should come over and swim in the pool sometime when it gets warmer."

"Yeah?" said Oggie. "*Prrrrr-ip! Prrrrr-ip!* That'd be cool!"

Turk, hearing Oggie's *prrrrr-ip*, let out a happy bark. Then he continued his pursuit of a large pink-

and-white inflatable beach ball that had blown into the pool.

"So anyway, Oggie," Donnica said, twisting a piece of her golden hair around her finger as she spoke, "the reason I wanted to talk to you was because I was wondering if I could ask you a teensy-weensy little favor."

"A favor?" Oggie replied. "Sure."

"It's about that cheese thing you were doing out on your porch."

"Charving, you mean?"

"Whatever you call it, I want to know if you can teach me how to do it."

Oggie was so delighted he had to *prrrrr-ip* again. Turk didn't bark this time. He'd finally managed to catch the beach ball and in the process had popped it, so he had a mouth full of soggy pink-and-white plastic at the moment.

"Maybe when it gets warmer and I come over to swim in your pool I could bring some cheese and my atlas and we could practice together," he said.

"Um, I don't think you understand." Donnica was getting impatient. "I need you to teach me how to do it today. Actually, like, right now."

"Now? Oh, I'm sorry, I can't. I have to help my mom at the store this afternoon."

"But you *have* to, Oggie. *Pleeeeeeease*," whined Donnica. "If you don't teach me right away I won't have enough time to practice before tomorrow afternoon."

"What's happening tomorrow afternoon?"

Donnica realized too late that she had painted herself into a corner. If she told Oggie about the contest he might decide to enter it himself. She certainly couldn't have that. *Think fast*, she told herself.

"Okay. See, I have to do a birthday party for, um, Dawn's little sister," she said. "They were supposed to have a clown, but he canceled at the last minute. So I said I'd do it. And I don't know how to make balloon animals or do magic tricks or anything, so I was thinking . . ."

"You want to *charve* for them?" said Oggie.

"Yeah. Why not? Little kids love cheese, right?"

"I guess," Oggie said.

"So will you teach me?" asked Donnica. "*Now*?"

"I told you already, I can't do it right now. Unless —"

"Unless what?"

"Unless you want to come down to the store with me. You could charve while I sort shoes."

Donnica swallowed hard. "You mean go *inside* your parents' store? With *you*?" she said uneasily.

"Yeah, we've got plenty of cheese in our fridge," said Oggie. "I'll go put Turk inside and grab some slices. Get your bike and I'll meet you back out here in a minute."

Donnica didn't see any way around it. If she wanted to impress the *Hidden Talents* judges, she was going to have to do whatever it took to make it happen. Even if it meant going with Oggie Cooder to his parents' creepy old junk shop to learn how to charve.

A minute later, Donnica was wheeling her bike out of the garage. As she hopped on, a gust of wind blew through the neighborhood, strong enough to make the bike wobble underneath her. Donnica grabbed the handlebars tighter. Oggie was already waiting for her at the bottom of the driveway. He grinned and waved, then he sniffed and wiped his nose with the back of his hand.

"Dis —" she muttered, as she pedaled toward him. This time she finished her own word, "— gusting."

If only Donnica had looked up, she might have noticed the curtains fluttering in the open window as the wind slipped past them into her room and caught the edge of the pink flyer, lifting it up off the bed where she'd left it and carrying it swiftly away.

10

oo Good to Be Threw was about a ten-minute ride away. Every time a car passed, Donnica would duck her head and tuck her chin into her shoulder to make sure that nobody recognized her. When she and Oggie arrived at the store, they rested their bikes next to each other against the wall. Then Oggie pushed open the door, setting a string of brass bells jingling a cheerful welcome overhead.

"Sorry, we're closed for inventory!" Mrs. Cooder called from the back of the store. "And on top of that, we're leaking!"

"It's me, Mom!" Oggie shouted back. "And Donnica!"

"Donnica Perfecto?" said Mrs. Cooder, pushing her way through a rack of old fur coats and emerging with a moth-eaten sleeve caught around her neck like a one-armed bear hug. "This *is* a surprise."

Mrs. Cooder was wearing a long purple dress with white polka dots. Around her waist she had tied a wide lavender-striped necktie. In her hand she held a child-size felt cowboy hat with a faded picture of a freckle-faced boy on the front. The words HOWDY DOODY were stitched under it.

"Donnica asked me to teach her how to charve," Oggie said, holding up the atlas and the package of cheese he'd brought with him.

"Oh, dear. I was counting on you to do the shoes." Mrs. Cooder pointed to a mountain of old footwear sitting in a heap on the floor. "Your dad's off trying to chase down another plumber, and I've got to move all the hats away from that back wall, because of the leak. Poor Howdy here nearly went for a swim." Mrs. Cooder gently brushed off the cowboy hat. "I really need your help, Ogg."

"Don't worry, I can do both, Mom," Oggie promised.

"Great," said Mrs. Cooder, untangling herself from the coat. "You know the drill. Anything without a mate, toss in the throwaway box."

Donnica looked around and wondered why they didn't just toss the whole place in the throwaway box.

Mrs. Cooder left Oggie and Donnica and returned to the task of rescuing her hats.

"You sit here," Oggie said, getting a chair for Donnica and putting it next to the shoe mountain. "I'll get you started, and then I can match shoes while you practice charving."

Oggie spent about ten minutes showing Donnica the basics.

"It's all about taking little bites," he told her. "Start with Kansas. Kansas, Wyoming, and Colorado are the easiest."

Donnica opened the atlas on her lap and peeled the wrapper off a fresh piece of cheese. For the next hour they worked side-by-side, Donnica charving and Oggie digging through the old shoes looking for matches. Every now and then, Donnica would stop and ask Oggie for his opinion.

"How's this?" she'd say, holding up a lopsided, chewed-up piece of cheese.

"Horrible," Oggie would answer honestly. Then he would put down the shoe he was holding and take a fresh piece of cheese out of the package.

"You need to take smaller bites," he'd tell her. Or, "It helps if you tilt your head when you go around the curves. See?" Then he'd quickly nibble the cheese into a perfect Tennessee, or Oregon, or West Virginia.

"How come you're so good at it?" Donnica asked, tossing yet another mangled piece of cheese into the reject pile that was quickly growing at her feet.

"Practice makes perfect," he said. "But if it turns out that even after you practice you still stink at it, maybe you can buy a book of magic tricks and learn one of those instead."

"Why would I want to do that?" Donnica asked, peeling the cellophane wrapper off a fresh piece of cheese.

"For the party," said Oggie.

"Oh, right," Donnica said. "The party."

The bells on the front door jingled.

"Is that you, Dennis?" Mrs. Cooder called, thinking maybe her husband had returned.

"Uh, no," a woman's voice called back. "Sorry to bother you. I was just wondering if you might have any lamps for sale."

"We're closed for inventory right now," Mrs. Cooder answered. "Plus we've sprung a leak, but, well, come on in. I'll show you what we've got."

Mrs. Cooder came to the front of the store and escorted her customer to the furniture section.

"Sorry about the mess," Oggie overheard her saying. "Plumbing problems. Can you believe one measly pipe could cost ten thousand dollars to replace?"

"Ouch," said the woman sympathetically.

"Heaven knows where we're going to find that kind of money. A lamp, you said, right? How about this nice green one, or if you want something unusual, this kitten has a nose that lights up when you plug it in."

"Oh, that one would be perfect for my daughter's room," said the woman.

Oggie was busy pawing through the pile of shoes, looking for the match to a blue one with rhinestones on the straps, when he glanced up and saw Amy Schneider standing there watching him.

"Hi," he said.

Amy gave a little wave.

Donnica, who didn't want anyone to know what she was up to, was unhappy to see Amy. She quickly shoved the piece of cheese she'd been working on into her mouth, then hid the rest of the package behind her back.

"What are you doing here?" Oggie asked Amy.

"My mom's looking for a lamp," Amy answered softly.

"Oh, well, I'm matching shoes for my mom," Oggie told her, "and Donnica is —"

"Matching shoes, too," Donnica interrupted, quickly swallowing the lump of cheese in her mouth and then jumping off the chair to throw herself into a sudden frenzy of shoe sorting. "We're very busy, Annie."

"You mean Amy," corrected Oggie.

"Whatever," said Donnica. "The point is, we're very busy and there's not much room back here. And besides that, you know what they say about three being a crowd, right?"

Amy got the message loud and clear, but Oggie, as usual, missed the point and didn't understand that Donnica was trying to make Amy feel unwelcome.

"I can scooch over and make more room if you want to help, too," he said. He reached into the pile of shoes and pulled out a red one with a big flower on the toe. "Why don't you see if you can find the other one of these?"

But when he turned around to hand Amy the shoe, she was gone.

"I wonder where she disappeared to," he said.

Donnica shrugged and tried to look innocent.

A few minutes later, the bells jingled over the door as the Schneiders left with their purchase. Donnica immediately threw down the shoe she'd been pretending to find a match for and went to retrieve the package of cheese from its hiding place.

"Can't you lock the door, or something?" she said. "It's very distracting when people just show up uninvited like that. . . ."

In the car on the way home, Amy held the new kitten lamp on her lap.

"Won't that be cute in your room?" asked her mother.

"Uh-huh," said Amy, but her thoughts weren't on the lamp. Instead, she was picturing the sneaky look she'd seen on Donnica Perfecto's face and thinking —

I wonder what she's up to.

11

ater, when Mrs. Cooder came over to check on Oggie's progress with the shoes, Donnica was taking a break from her charving, busy putting nail polish on a pinkie nail, which she'd accidentally chipped on a shoe buckle.

"Dumb, dirty, disgusting old shoe," she muttered under her breath.

"If you're not too busy, Donnica," said Mrs. Cooder pleasantly, "maybe you'd like to give me a hand sorting through some of the dresses on the racks in the back."

"*Me?*" Donnica had no desire to touch clothes that total strangers had already worn.

"We have a lot of cute things. Who knows, you

might even find something you'd like to take home with you."

"You mean *to wear*?" Donnica said, unable to keep from shuddering. "Uh, thanks, Mrs. Cooder, but as soon as my nail dries I really have to get back to practicing. I *have* to learn how to charve today. It's a matter of life and death."

"Life and death?" Mrs. Cooder raised her eyebrows. "That sounds pretty serious."

"Donnica is going to charve at a birthday party tomorrow," Oggie explained.

Donnica couldn't help blushing when she heard her lie repeated.

"Must be a very important birthday party," said Mrs. Cooder, taking note of Donnica's bubble-gum-pink cheeks.

Amy Schneider was not the only one thinking, *I wonder what she's up to.*

The bells over the door jingled again. This time it was the pizza being delivered. "*Prrrrr-ip!*" cried Oggie in happy anticipation.

Donnica wouldn't have minded a slice of pizza herself right then, but when she peered into the cardboard box, she gasped.

"What is that yellow and pink stuff all over it?"

"Pineapple and ham," said Oggie.

"On a *pizza*?"

"Yeppers," Oggie told her. "It's my favorite."

Donnica was about to say something snotty like, "Why am I not surprised that your favorite pizza would be covered with something gross and disgusting that nobody else would want to go near?" But she bit her tongue, reminding herself that she wasn't quite finished with Oggie yet.

"Can you show me again how to make my edges smoother?" she asked as soon as Oggie was done with his pizza. "Mine still look too jaggedy."

At 5:30 Mrs. Cooder turned out the lights and locked up the store.

"Thanks for your help," she said, giving Oggie's shoulder a squeeze. "I'll see you at home. You two ride carefully now, it's starting to get dark."

Oggie and Donnica got their bikes.

"Do you want me to come over later tonight, after I finish my homework?" Oggie asked as they started pedaling along next to each other.

"Why would I want you to do that?" Donnica couldn't imagine actually inviting Oggie to come inside her house.

"So I could help you with your charving," Oggie said. "Your edges are still pretty jaggedy, you know."

"I just need to practice."

"Maybe I could give you some more tips. Like you should tilt your head when you do curves."

Donnica sighed. "You already told me that."

"And you should take small bites."

"You told me that already, too," said Donnica. "Tell the truth — is there anything you haven't taught me yet?"

Oggie had a feeling there was something he had forgotten to tell her, but he couldn't for the life of him think of what it could be.

"I guess maybe I've taught you everything I know," he said.

"That's what I thought," said Donnica, then she stood up and began to pedal harder, quickly pulling ahead of Oggie's bike.

"Hey, wait up," called Oggie. "Where are you going in such a hurry?"

"Hollywood!" Donnica shouted at the top of her lungs, then she rounded the corner and disappeared from sight.

12

The following day, Donnica stayed home from school, pretending to be sick.

Mrs. Perfecto brought her daughter tea and toast in bed.

"Is there anything else I can get you, Cupcake?" Mrs. Perfecto asked.

"Uh-huh." Donnica nodded weakly. "More cheese."

Mrs. Perfecto couldn't believe how much cheese her daughter was eating all of a sudden. What was going on? Had she come down with some kind of strange cheese disease? "You've already had a whole package this morning," she pointed out. "Are you sure you want more?"

"I WANT MORE CHEESE," demanded Donnica.

"Yes, Cupcake, right away," said Mrs. Perfecto, hurrying out of the room.

While Mr. Snolinovsky's fourth-grade class did math and spelling and watched a nature video about the Galápagos Islands, Donnica Perfecto spent the morning hiding under her covers, charving cheese. Once when she was lost in concentration trying to perfect the thumb on the lower peninsula of Michigan, she failed to hear her mother approaching and was nearly caught in the act. Fortunately, at the last second, Donnica heard the doorknob turn and managed to toss the evidence *up* — which is how she discovered that cheese sticks very nicely to a plaster ceiling if you throw it hard enough.

Meanwhile, at Truman Elementary, Donnica's absence did not go unnoticed.

"Maybe she really *was* sick yesterday," Dawn said to Hannah as they sat at lunch together, both feeling at a bit of a loss. They didn't know what to do, with no one there to boss them around or to pro-vide first syllables for them to finish.

Oggie, who was sitting across from Amy, eating a piece of cold pizza left over from the day before, was wondering about Donnica, too.

"She seemed okay when we rode home yester-day from the store," he told Amy, as he picked off a piece of pineapple and popped it in his mouth.

Amy, who hadn't been able to shake the feeling that Donnica was up to something, began pulling off her rubber bands and dropping them one by one onto her napkin.

"Did I tell you that she invited me to come swim in her pool this summer?" Oggie continued.

Amy nodded and, having removed the last of her rubber bands, took an unencumbered bite of her tuna fish sandwich. Oggie had told her about the pool invitation twice since they'd sat down to lunch.

Oggie went on. "They've got this cabana banana thing which is full of towels in case anybody needs one. Isn't that cool?"

Amy nodded. She'd already heard about the cabana banana, too. What she couldn't figure out (and was too shy to ask) was how Donnica and Oggie had suddenly become such good friends. Amy had seen her making fun of Oggie behind his back plenty of times. Why was Donnica hanging out with him now?

"Hey," said Oggie, "I just thought of something. Since Donnica is sick, maybe she'll need somebody to fill in for her at the birthday party this afternoon."

This was the first time Amy had heard anything about a birthday party.

"Whose birthday is it?" she asked.

"Dawn's little sister," Oggie told her. "Donnica's going to charve for the kids, since the clown couldn't come."

"Donnica knows how to *charve*?" Amy asked.

"Yeppers. I taught her how yesterday."

Amy was more convinced than ever that something *extremely* fishy was going on.

*   *   *

That afternoon in class, Mr. Snolinovsky brought out an old record player that had belonged to him when he was a kid. He'd also brought along some special records. There were pictures of cowboys on the covers, some of them with fiddles tucked under their chins, others in bright red snap shirts holding guitars.

"When I was a boy, we used to square-dance at school," he told the class. "Every Friday, at the end of the day, we'd push all the desks to one side of the room, bow to our partners, and allemande left, do-si-do, and promenade until we were red in the face. I loved it so much I thought I might try introducing you to the joys of square dancing, too."

You could have heard a pin drop.

"We gotta dance?" asked David Korben, finally breaking the silence.

"With partners?" whispered Bethie Hudson, her big blues eyes wide in horror.

Oggie was the only one other than Mr. Snolinovsky who thought square dancing sounded like fun. His parents had an antique windup

Victrola in the living room at home, and sometimes they would crank it up and dance. Oggie loved to watch his parents twirl around in each other's arms. His mother had taught him a few steps, but Oggie always seemed to trip over his own feet and end up stepping on her toes.

"Make two lines, one for boys, one for girls, and go from tallest to smallest," Mr. Snolinovsky told the class.

There were twelve girls and eleven boys in the class, but since Donnica was absent, it worked out evenly. Oggie was the next-to-tallest boy in the line, and as it happened, Dawn was the next-to-tallest girl — so they were partners. As Oggie followed Mr. Snolinovsky's directions, taking Dawn by the arm and escorting her to their corner of the square, Dawn shot a look of total despair toward Hannah. Hannah was paired up with Jackson Polito, who she secretly thought was kind of cute, so she wasn't as unhappy about her partner as Dawn was.

Mr. Snolinovsky put on one of the scratchy records, and pretty soon they were square-dancing.

Or at least trying to. Oggie did his best to follow the instructions, hooking elbows with Dawn and skipping around in a circle when the caller told them to "swing your partners!" But it wasn't long before the inevitable happened.

"Ouch!" Dawn cried, suddenly grabbing her foot and hopping around on one leg. "You stepped on me!"

"Oops. Sorry!" said Oggie.

Mr. Snolinovsky told them to sit the next one out so Dawn's foot could have a chance to recover. Oggie sat beside her on the floor while the others continued dancing. There was a lot of complaining going on, but it actually seemed like most of the kids were having fun, even if they didn't want to admit it.

After a while, Oggie leaned toward Dawn and shouted over the music, "You must be excited, huh?"

"About what? Getting stomped on?" Dawn said, scowling as she rubbed her sore foot.

"No," Oggie said. "About the party this afternoon."

"What party?" asked Dawn.

"Your sister's party."

Now Dawn was *really* confused. "I don't have a sister," she said. "I'm an only child."

"That's weird," said Oggie. "Donnica told me she was going to be helping out at your sister's birthday party today. I spent the whole afternoon with her yesterday teaching her everything I know. Or at least I *think* I taught her everything. There might be something I forgot, but I can't remember what it —"

Dawn cut him off.

"Let me get this straight," she said. "You were with Donnica yesterday after school?"

"Yeppers. She came to the store with me."

"*She did?* How did she seem?"

"Fine," said Oggie. "Except her edges were a little jaggedy."

"What about her appendix — was it exploding?"

"I don't think so," said Oggie.

"Hmmmm," said Dawn.

And someone else was added to the growing list of people wondering what in the world Donnica Perfecto was up to.

13

At 2:30 Friday afternoon, as the sweaty square dancers in Mr. Snolinovsky's class pushed their desks back into place and got ready for dismissal, Donnica Perfecto was sneaking out her back door clutching the handle of a minicooler containing several slices of American cheese. She had stuffed pillows under her covers in case her mother came into her room to check on her. Since she was afraid of running into anyone she knew — especially Dawn and Hannah — she'd left herself enough time to ride her bike the back way to the Wawatosa Bandshell.

The weather was beautiful that day, sunny and warm, with none of the gusty winds from the previous day, which had blown the lids off garbage cans and sent all manner of things fluttering and scuttering around the neighborhood.

Hannah and Dawn were standing on the corner, waiting for the light to change, when Oggie Cooder came up behind them. Instead of ignoring him, the way they usually would have, Dawn turned around and faced Oggie.

"Tell Hannah what you told me about Donnica saying she had to go to my little sister's birthday party today."

"That's what she said," Oggie reported. "She told me the clown was sick."

"How weird is that?" said Dawn.

"Very," said Hannah. "She told us yesterday she was going straight home to bed because her appendix was about to explode. But you said her appendix was fine, right, Oggie?"

"Yeppers," nodded Oggie.

"I think maybe it's time for us to go pay her a little visit," Dawn said.

When the three of them reached Tullahoma Street, Hannah and Dawn crossed over to go to the Perfectos' house to confront Donnica, while Oggie continued on home. He knew Turk would be eagerly awaiting his afternoon walk.

A few minutes later, Oggie emerged from the house with Turk on his leash. As usual, Turk had a spitty yellow tennis ball in his mouth and his tail was wagging like a flag. The afternoon walk was his favorite, because often Oggie would take him to the park and throw the ball for him. Oggie glanced across the street, but there was no sign of Hannah or Dawn. He considered going over there himself to tell Donnica that the next time she wanted him to do her a favor, she didn't have to make up some crazy story to get him to do it. He was happy to help her in any way he could — especially now that she'd invited him to come swimming in her pool.

Turk started tugging on his leash so hard that Oggie's shoulder felt like it was about to pop.

"Okay, okay, I get the message," he said. "Here we go."

On the corner, Turk stopped to inspect a large bush popular with the neighborhood dogs. While Turk nosed around in the branches, Oggie turned back to look down the block at the Perfectos' house once more. This time, Hannah and Dawn were standing out on the sidewalk. They waved for him to come over to where they were.

"Donnica's disappeared!" Hannah told him.

"Disappeared?" said Oggie.

"Yeah, her mom is really worried. She said Donnica was acting totally weird today."

"Yeah, like she couldn't stop eating cheese. And now she's missing," said Dawn.

Oggie was about to explain that Donnica might not have actually been *eating* the cheese, she might have been *charving* it — though he was still a little unclear about why she'd want to do that if she wasn't really planning to charve at a birthday party. But any thoughts about Donnica Perfecto and cheese were suddenly lost as Oggie looked down and noticed something that greatly alarmed him. The yellow tennis ball in Turk's mouth had turned a very bright shade of pink. At first he was worried that Turk might have cut his mouth on something, but when he pulled the ball out, he discovered it wasn't a ball at all, but rather a crumpled-up piece of pink paper.

"He must have found it in the bushes," Oggie said, relieved. Then something occurred to him. "You know what?" he said. "This paper looks like the exact same shade of pink as the flyer I saw that guy putting up on the bulletin board at school yesterday."

"What guy?" Dawn asked.

"What flyer?" asked Hannah.

Oggie uncrumpled the soggy paper. It was the very same flyer Donnica had pulled off the bulletin board the day before. The wind had snatched it off her bed and carried it down the street, where it had become snagged in the bush.

"Yeppers! This is it, all right. See? It says: 'three pm at The Wawatosa Bandshell.' That's exactly what he told me."

He held the paper out for the others to see. Dawn and Hannah's mouths fell open.

"*Hidden Talents*!" they exclaimed in unison.

"What's that?" asked Oggie.

"It's only the hottest show on TV right now," Dawn explained.

"Everybody watches it," Hannah added.

Everybody but Oggie. He'd never even heard of *Hidden Talents*, which was not all that surprising considering that the Cooders didn't own a television set. Mr. and Mrs. Cooder firmly believed that microwave ovens, hair spray, diet soda, and television were all very bad for your brain cells, so they didn't allow any of those things in their home.

"Donnica's not missing," said Hannah, looking carefully at the flyer.

"She's not?" asked Dawn.

"No," Hannah said. "And she's not sick, either."

"Then where is she?" asked Oggie.

"She's *auditioning*," said Hannah.

"Why didn't she tell us about the audition?" Dawn sounded hurt.

"Probably because she was afraid we might beat her," said Hannah. "What time is it, anyway?"

Oggie looked at his watch. "Ten after three."

The front door opened and Mrs. Perfecto came rushing out of the house with her car keys in her hand.

"I've got to go look for my Cupcake," she cried.

"We've got a pretty good idea about where she is," Dawn told her.

"You do? Oh, thank goodness!" Mrs. Perfecto put her hand over her heart. She opened the side door of the SUV.

"Jump in. You can help me find her. Oh, I hope she's all right!"

"She may not be once I get my hands on her," muttered Dawn as she and Hannah climbed into the car.

Oggie wasn't sure if he was invited, too, but Turk, who loved nothing better than a ride in the car, bounded into the backseat, dragging Oggie along with him.

Five minutes later, Mrs. Perfecto was turning into the parking lot of the Bandshell.

"Are you sure this is where she is?" she asked.

Oggie looked across the lawn at the small crowd gathered in front of the stage.

"There she is!" he said, pointing at a figure in pink corduroy overalls, standing on the side of the stage pacing nervously.

"Cupcake!" cried Mrs. Perfecto.

"What's she holding?" asked Hannah, squinting at Donnica as she tried to make out what was in her hand.

"Looks like a book," said Dawn. "Or maybe a CD."

But Oggie shook his head. He knew exactly what it was.

"Cheese," he told them all.

14

As the four of them got out of the car and hurried toward the Bandshell, Mrs. Perfecto and the two girls peppered Oggie with enough questions so that by the time they reached the stage they were all aware of what Donnica was planning to do with the piece of cheese in her hand.

"She's stealing your talent, Oggie," someone said softly.

But it wasn't Mrs. Perfecto or Dawn or Hannah who said it. It was Amy Schneider.

"Where did you come from?" Oggie asked, surprised.

"I had a feeling Donnica was up to no good," Amy told him. "So when I saw her ride by my house on her bike a little while ago, I followed her here. I just hope we're not too late."

"Too late for what?" asked Oggie.

"To stop her."

"Next!" cried a small bald man with a large megaphone.

"Hey! That's the flyer guy," said Oggie, pointing to the man.

Donnica walked out onto the stage and stood in front of the judges, who were sitting in a row of metal folding chairs behind a long table.

"State your name and your hidden talent for the judges, please," the man with the megaphone said.

Donnica flashed the judges her biggest, brightest smile.

"My name is Donnica Perfecto and my hidden talent is *charving*."

"Excuse me? Did you say *carving*?" asked one of the judges leaning forward.

"No," said Donnica. "*Charving*. It's a combination of chewing and carving."

"Quirky," said the judge, nodding approvingly.

Donnica flashed another smile.

"Aren't you going to stop her?" asked Amy, giving Oggie a little nudge toward the stage.

"Why would I do that?"

"Because she stole your talent," said Amy.

"No, she didn't," said Oggie. "I taught her how to charve."

"But she tricked you," Hannah chimed in.

"And she lied to us," added Dawn.

"Doesn't she look lovely?" sighed Mrs. Perfecto, who seemed to have completely forgotten that only minutes ago she'd been worried sick about her daughter's whereabouts.

"Quiet, please!" the man shouted at the crowd through his megaphone. Then he turned back to Donnica and said, "You're on, kid."

Donnica flashed that smile again, then she lifted the cheese to her lips dramatically.

"Wisconsin!" she announced. But before she'd even taken a bite, she stopped.

"Something's not right," she said, looking at the cheese. "There's something wrong with this piece. It's *sticky*."

"Too warm," Oggie told Amy. "She shouldn't have held it in her hand for so long before she started."

"Hang on," Donnica told the judges. "I'll get another piece."

She ran over to the side of the stage where she'd stashed her minicooler. Flipping it open, she quickly grabbed a fresh slice of cheese, tore off the cellophane wrapper with her teeth, and hurried back to her spot.

"Wisconsin!" she announced again. But this time when she bit into the cheese, it cracked in half.

"Too cold," said Oggie.

"What's happening?" asked Mrs. Perfecto nervously.

"Justice," whispered Dawn.

"Yeah," agreed Hannah with a satisfied smile.

The man with the megaphone was growing

impatient. "Sorry, kid," he said. "Your time's up. We've got a schedule to keep to here. Who's next?"

Amy was relieved that Donnica wasn't going to get away with her little plan, but when she turned to Oggie to tell him so, she found he wasn't standing next to her anymore. Looking up, she was surprised to see him running out onto the stage.

"Hey, Donnica!" Oggie shouted as he sprinted across the stage, pulling Turk along behind him on his leash. "I finally remembered what I forgot to tell you before. The cheese has to be the right temperature!" He pulled a slice of cheese out of his back pocket and waved it in the air. "Like this one!"

"Gimme that!" screamed Donnica, reaching for the cheese with a desperate look in her eyes.

But as Oggie ran past the judge's table, Turk caught a whiff of the crusts of a roast beef sandwich one of them had left lying on a paper plate after lunch, and he took a sudden unexpected detour. Oggie tripped over the leash and his feet came out from under him, causing him to fall just as he reached Donnica.

"Ooomph!"

"Youch!"

The two collided, bumping heads so hard they both saw stars and landed in a tangle of arms and legs on the stage.

Donnica's processed American ticket to Hollywood flew out of Oggie's hand, sailing high up into the air. It looked like the audition was over, but then to everyone's amazement, Donnica managed to untangle herself in time to leap up and catch the cheese a split second before it hit the floor.

"Wait!" she shouted, rushing back to face the judges.

The man with the megaphone took pity on her. "One last chance, kid."

"With-consin!" said Donnica, holding up the cheese.

Dawn looked at Hannah. "Is it my imagination, or did she just say '*With*-consin'?"

15

Thanks to the perfect climate in Oggie's back pocket, the cheese finally cooperated. Donnica felt certain that the judges would be impressed by Wisconsin, and so she had practiced it many times up in her room. Now she closed her eyes to help her concentrate, and carefully began to nibble the cheese, taking tiny bites and tilting her head as she went around the curves, just the way Oggie had taught her.

Oggie stayed right where he was, afraid if he got up and left in the middle of Donnica's performance it might distract the judges or, worse, mess Donnica up. In the excitement, Turk had managed to grab the sandwich crusts and run off with them. To Oggie's relief, he saw that Amy had caught Turk before he'd gotten very far and was holding tight to his leash now.

As he watched Donnica charve, Oggie could tell that she'd been practicing because she was much more confident than she'd been the day before. The judges leaned forward with great interest. They seemed to be enjoying it. Oggie felt proud of his pupil. Then as Donnica turned the cheese in her hands, Oggie caught a glimpse of what looked like a very jaggedy edge and suddenly he felt nervous for her. Without thinking about it, he did what he always did when he felt nervous. He reached into his back pocket, pulled out the remaining slice of cheese, and began to charve to calm his nerves.

Donnica finished, opened her eyes, and held up her cheese triumphantly. Oggie's heart sank when he saw it. Just as he'd suspected, it was jaggedy. Really jaggedy. In fact, it was the worst job of charving he'd ever seen her do. But while he was sitting there feeling sorry for her, the judges suddenly broke into enthusiastic applause.

"First-rate!"

"Dynamite talent!"

"Quirky with a capital *Q*!" one of them exclaimed enthusiastically.

"Fank you," said Donnica, taking a bow.

This time it was Hannah who looked at Dawn. "*Fank* you?"

"No, no, not you, honey," one of the judges said to Donnica. "We're talking about *him*."

Shocked, Donnica whirled around on her heel to see who they were pointing at . . . and there was Oggie Cooder holding a perfectly charved Texas in his hand. Donnica was so angry her face turned a shade of purple Mrs. Cooder would have called *eggplant*.

"Thath not fair!" she wailed. "I wath thuppothed to be the one audithioning."

There was a sudden gasp from the audience as Mrs. Perfecto pointed at Donnica with a shaking finger.

"Your teeth, Cupcake! What's happened to your beautiful teeth?"

Donnica quickly put her fingers up to her mouth.

No wonder the charving had been off! She had chipped both of her front teeth when she and Oggie had bumped heads! Needless to say, she was furious.

"I won't forget thith, Oggie Cooder!" she shouted before she ran off the stage.

Mrs. Perfecto quickly whisked Donnica away in the SUV for an emergency dental appointment with Dr. Schelkun. Oggie felt terrible. He hadn't meant to ruin Donnica's audition. He even tried to persuade the judges to give her another chance.

"Maybe she could come back tomorrow and charve for you after she gets her teeth fixed," he said. "She's usually much better than that, and she's been practicing a lot."

"There's only one slot left for the next show, and we have to fill it today," they told Oggie.

"But —" said Oggie.

"Sorry kid," said the man with the megaphone.

So Oggie, feeling miserable and guilty, slunk off the stage.

"Thanks for watching Turk," he said as Amy handed him back the leash. "I guess I'd better get going."

"You can't leave now," Amy told him.

"Why not?" said Oggie.

"Because you don't know yet whether you won," she answered.

"I never win anything," Oggie said. "And I didn't even mean to audition, I was just charving because I felt nervous for Donnica."

Up on the stage, Mr. Megaphone gestured to a boy with a large, white rabbit under his arm.

"You're next, kid. State your name and your talent for the judges, please."

"My name is Fred McMinnville, and I can make my rabbit faint," the boy told them.

The judges smiled and nodded their approval.

Fred set the rabbit down on the stage, crouched down beside it, and blew in its face. The rabbit instantly fell over in a dead faint.

Turk started barking so excitedly that Oggie had

to shush him. One of the judges asked Fred how he'd done the trick.

"Onion breath," he said, pulling a large red onion out of his pocket and taking a big bite of it. "Works every time."

"That was a pretty neat trick," Oggie said to Amy. "I wonder if it would work on Turk."

Next up was a little redheaded girl with a jar of olives in her hand.

"I can tap dance and eat olives at the same time," she announced proudly.

The judges didn't seem all that impressed, but Turk loved her because she kept dropping the olives, which he would gobble down as they rolled off the edge of the stage. One by one, kids came out and did strange, quirky things. There was a boy who could make his ears disappear by folding them up and tucking them inside his ear holes, and a tall skinny girl who could pop balloons with her shoulder blades. There were a number of kids who did tricks with hula hoops, including one girl who nearly choked herself by putting the hoop around her neck and trying to keep it going while she did an impression of the sound of a toilet flushing. When the last of the auditions were over, the judges bent their heads together and began to whisper. After a while, they called Fred back up and asked whether the fainting rabbit trick really worked every time.

"Well, almost every time," he said. "Sometimes, though, he just sneezes."

"Where's the kid with the cheese?" called the man with the megaphone.

"See? I told you," said Amy excitedly.

Oggie was called up onto the stage and asked whether Texas was the only state he could charve. Oggie didn't want to brag, but of course he told the truth, admitting that he could do all fifty.

"How about instead of one particular state, if we asked you to charve the entire country, do you think you could do that?" said one of the judges.

Oggie thought for a second.

"Well, I've never done it before," he said. "But I'm willing to give it a try. There's one problem though —" Oggie patted his back pocket. "I'm out of cheese."

It was Amy who noticed the minicooler Donnica had left behind. She ran and got a slice of cheese out of it and brought it to Oggie. He made sure to warm it up a little before he began to charve.

A minute later, everyone was very impressed when Oggie held up a perfectly executed U.S. of A.

Again the judges bent their heads together and whispered. This time they came to a decision.

"Pack your cheese, Oggie Cooder. You're going to Hollywood!"

16

What happened after that was all kind of a blur. News traveled fast, and the next morning Oggie's face was on the front page of the Wawatosa newspaper with the headline "LOCAL BOY BECOMES BIG CHEESE!" A television crew was outside on the Cooders' front lawn when Oggie came out to take Turk for his morning walk. Reporters began firing questions at him.

"How old were you when you first started charving?"

"When do you leave for Hollywood?"

"What are you going to do with the money?"

"What money?" asked Oggie.

"Didn't anyone tell you?" said one of the reporters. "Everybody who goes on the show gets ten thousand dollars. And if you win the whole she-bang, well, then we're talking *really* big bucks."

"Ten thousand dollars?" said Oggie. "Are you sure about that?"

"That's right. Ten thou."

"*Prrrrr-ip! Prrrrr-ip!*" cried Oggie happily, because he knew *exactly* what he was going to do with the money.

By noon, Oggie had received calls from a dozen different cheese companies asking if he'd be willing to use their product when he went on the show. Oggie's Aunt Hettie called to congratulate him and to say she'd always known he was destined for greatness. The Cooders were very proud of their son, and Mrs. Cooder carefully glued the newspaper clipping about Oggie into the scrapbook. Oggie had entered more contests than he could count, but this was the first time he had ever won anything. He should have been *prrrrr-ip*ing happily all over the place. But the one problem was — he felt bad about Donnica.

The Cooders had called the Perfectos immediately when they heard about Donnica's teeth, insisting on paying half of the dental bills. But Oggie knew that Donnica's chipped teeth were only part of the reason she was mad at him. She had wanted to win herself, and even though she had tricked Oggie into teaching her how to charve, he still felt guilty that he was the one who was going to be going to Hollywood. He wished he could think of something he could do to make it up to her, but so far the only idea he'd come up with was to crochet her a pair of shoelaces, which he planned to do as soon as he could get his hands on some pink yarn.

Later that day, Oggie was out in the garage pumping up his bicycle tires, when a shadow fell across the floor. At first, he thought maybe it was another reporter coming to ask him more questions, but when he looked up, there was Donnica Perfecto.

"Oh, hi," said Oggie. "How are your teeth feeling?"

"I'm not here to talk about my teeth," Donnica told him. There was a gleam in her eye that made Oggie feel uncomfortable.

She wasn't a big girl, but Donnica looked pretty strong. Oggie thought there was a distinct possibility that he was about to get flattened.

"Are you ready, Oggie Cooder?" Donnica asked.

"Not really," Oggie answered truthfully.

"Well, get ready, because when I'm done with you, even your own mother's not going to be able to recognize you."

Donnica Perfecto did not flatten Oggie in his garage that afternoon. What she did do was offer him a deal.

"I'll forgive you for what you did if you let me be your manager."

Truthfully, Oggie had no idea what a manager might do, but he didn't care. As soon as he heard the word "forgive," he was sold on the idea.

"*Prrrrr-ip! Prrrrr-ip!*" he said, relieved to be off the hook.

"I'm going to assume that ridiculous noise you're making means we have a deal," said Donnica.

"Yeppers!" agreed Oggie happily. "And now I don't even have to find pink yarn!"

When Oggie Cooder walked into Mr. Snolinovsky's classroom on Monday morning, everybody was excited to see him. People who didn't normally even say hello came running over to clap him on the back.

"I saw you in the newspaper!"

"Everybody's talking about you!"

"Hey, Oggie," giggled America Johnson, holding out two pieces of paper she had ripped from her notebook. "Can I have your autograph? One for me and one for my sister?"

Donnica jumped in before Oggie could answer.

"No autographs," she commanded. "And no pictures."

"Says who?" asked America.

"Says me," Donnica answered.

"Who made you boss?" David Korben asked.

"*He* did," said Donnica, jerking a thumb in Oggie's direction. "Right, Oggie?"

Oggie shrugged his shoulders and grinned. He couldn't believe how much his life had changed all because of one little piece of cheese.

At lunch, Donnica insisted that Oggie sit with her at the table by the window.

"Hurry up and eat," she said as Oggie unwrapped his sandwich. "We need to practice."

Donnica had taken to carrying a stopwatch with her so she could time Oggie when he practiced his charving.

"I still don't understand why I have to do it fast," Oggie said. "I didn't do it fast at the audition."

"You want to win, don't you?" Donnica told him.

Oggie nodded.

"You know that kid I told you about who won last year?" Donnica continued. "The one who could play 'The Star-Spangled Banner' with his armpit? Well, you wouldn't believe how fast he did it. And the judges *loved* him. And the kid who cracked the walnuts with his toes? He might have won instead if somebody had told him to speed it up a little. Now hurry up and finish your lunch — we've got work to do."

Having no interest any longer in being anywhere near Donnica Perfecto, Dawn and Hannah joined Amy at Oggie's old table over by the garbage cans. The three girls watched Donnica fussing over Oggie.

"Can you believe it?" Dawn said. "A few days ago she was calling him a loser, and now she's acting like she owns him or something."

"I can't believe we used to like her," said Hannah. "She's so fake."

"Yeah, like why is she helping Oggie try to win?" Dawn wondered. "We were her best friends and she didn't even tell us about the audition."

Amy didn't say anything. She just looked across the room at Oggie and shook her head. He wasn't the only one having a hard time believing how much that piece of cheese had changed things.

17

"here are your glasses?" Donnica asked Oggie as they walked down the hall to the classroom after lunch.

"In my pocket," Oggie answered.

"Put them on," Donnica said, snapping her fingers at him.

"But they're sunglasses," he pointed out.

"Trust me, people in Hollywood always wear sunglasses, even when they're inside."

"But we're not in Hollywood."

Donnica gave him her *don't cross me* look, something Oggie had been seeing quite a lot of since Donnica had become his manager. In order to avoid a confrontation, he put the sunglasses on.

David and a couple of his jock buddies sidled over to them.

"Hey, Oggie," David said. "How about playing a little B-ball with us after school? Maybe the newspaper will come and take our pictures."

Oggie was thrilled.

"Prrrrr-ip! Prrrrr-ip!"

"STOP *prrrrr-ip*ing!" Donnica demanded, grabbing Oggie's arm. "How many times do I have to tell you, that noise is annoying and weird. Trust me, Hollywood does not like annoying and weird."

"What about it, Oggie? Want to play ball with us?" asked David again. "You don't have to listen to everything old bossy face says."

"Oh, yes, he does!" said Donnica. "And there is absolutely no way he can play basketball this afternoon."

"Why not?" Oggie asked, dismayed.

"A, we have too much work to do. And B, you might do something cloddy, like run into somebody and chip your teeth," Donnica told Oggie pointedly.

So Oggie reluctantly declined an invitation he'd basically been waiting for his whole life.

After school, Donnica insisted that Oggie go with her to Selznick's department store.

"You need some new clothes," she told him.

"What's wrong with the clothes I've already got?" asked Oggie.

"You want to win, don't you?" said Donnica. "Trust me, your clothes are too weird. And one other thing — you know that silly word you always say instead of yes?"

"You mean 'yeppers'?" said Oggie. "What about it?"

"People in Hollywood don't say 'yeppers,' they just say yes. Understood?"

"Yes," said Oggie quietly, and he noticed the first small twinges of an uncomfortable pinching feeling in the pit of his stomach.

Donnica Perfectos' ideas about fashion boiled down to the complete opposite of everything Oggie had ever worn.

She picked out a pair of khaki pants and a navy blue polo shirt for him to try on.

"I like stripes," Oggie told her. "And checks, too."

"No stripes," said Donnica. "And absolutely no checks. Put these on and then we'll go look for shoes. You'll need brown ones to go with your pants."

"I've got some brown yarn," Oggie told Donnica. "Maybe I'll make some laces to go with my new shoes."

"You're not going to wear homemade shoelaces on the show," said Donnica.

"I'm not?" asked Oggie. He couldn't imagine wearing shoes without homemade laces in them.

"No," said Donnica, "because —"

"People in Hollywood don't wear crocheted shoelaces?" guessed Oggie.

"True," Donnica said, "but the main reason is because they look dumb."

Oggie was confused. "The other day you told me you loved them. Remember? You said, 'Love your shoelaces, Oggie Cooder.'"

"I was kidding," said Donnica as they turned the corner and started up Tullahoma Street.

Oggie put his hand on his stomach. That uncomfortable pinching feeling was getting a little bit stronger.

"What's the matter with you?" asked Donnica, noticing Oggie rubbing his stomach.

"I'm not sure," said Oggie. "You don't think my appendix is about to explode, do you?"

Donnica didn't answer. She was looking up the street at Oggie's house.

"Whose car is that in your driveway?" she asked.

Oggie told her he didn't recognize it.

"Well, if it's anybody important, call me," Donnica said. "And remember —"

"I know." Oggie sighed, rubbing his stomach again. "No autographs, no photographs, no basketball, no shoelaces, no nothing."

There were two men sitting in the living room with Mrs. Cooder when Oggie walked in. Turk came charging over to jump up on Oggie and give him a welcome-home face licking.

"So this is the famous Oggie Cooder everyone's been talking about," said the taller of the two men, rising in order to shake Oggie's hand. He had on blue jeans and a white shirt with the sleeves rolled up. On his feet he wore expensive-looking leather loafers and no socks. "I'm Bradley Mathis from *HT*."

"What's *HT*?" asked Oggie.

The man chuckled. "*Hidden Talents*. You have heard of the show, haven't you?"

"Actually none of us were familiar with your show until Oggie got chosen to be on it," said Mrs. Cooder, smoothing the front of her purple skirt with her hand. "You see, we don't own a television, Mr. Mathis."

Mr. Mathis looked stunned.

"Do you mean to say, you've never seen the show?" he asked Oggie.

"No, I haven't," said Oggie. "Does that mean I can't be on it?"

"Are you kidding?" exclaimed Mr. Mathis. "Our publicity people are going to *love* this!" He pulled a pen out of his pocket. "I've brought some contracts for you and your parents to sign, and Jimmy here is going to snap a few photos."

The other man unsnapped the black bag hanging from his shoulder and pulled out a camera.

"I'm not supposed to sign anything or have my picture taken without my manager here," said Oggie, remembering Donnica's rules. "And I can't play basketball with you, either."

"You have a manager?" Mr. Mathis seemed surprised. "That was fast. What agency?"

"It's just the neighbor girl," Mrs. Cooder explained. "She's taken a sudden and rather surprising interest in Oggie since you people came to town."

"Yeah," Oggie said, "she's the one who bought me these new clothes."

"I was wondering where those came from," said Mrs. Cooder, eyeing Oggie's crisp new khaki pants.

"Actually," said Mr. Mathis, "I was wondering about those clothes myself. Do you think I could talk to that manager of yours, Oggie?"

"Hang on," said Oggie. "I know how to get her over here fast."

He walked over to the window, pulled it open, and leaned out.

"DONNICA!" he shouted. "Somebody's trying to take my picture!"

Two seconds later, she was there.

18

Apparently, Donnica knew a lot less about Hollywood than she thought she did.

"We don't want you messing with his look anymore," Mr. Mathis told her. "We like the whole Oggie Cooder package — the clothes, the funny-looking dog, the weird noises, and especially those crazy shoelaces. And we think America is going to like it, too."

"Does that mean I can say 'yeppers' again, Mr. Mathis?" asked Oggie hopefully.

"Absolutely," said Mr. Mathis. "And forget the formality — we're a team now, Oggie. Please call me Brad."

"You know," said Mrs. Cooder, "now that I think of it, several kids came into the store yesterday, asking whether we had any seersucker pants. I wonder if that was because of Oggie."

Some of those kids were from Oggie's class, because over the next few days more and more of them showed up at Truman wearing things that had obviously come from the racks of Too Good to Be Threw.

The talk at Bethie Hudson's lunch table changed from horses to crocheting, and pretty soon all the girls were making homemade shoelaces just like Oggie's. Kids were getting into charving, too. Grocery stores in Wawatosa reported record sales of American cheese slices. The excitement about Oggie going to Hollywood was building to a fever pitch.

Donnica switched gears immediately and became as fierce about preserving Oggie's image as she had been about trying to change it.

"If any reporters show up, make sure you *prrrrr-ip* as much as possible," she'd tell him. "And toss in a couple of yeppers, too."

She also suggested that besides saying "yeppers," he add "nopers" to his vocabulary.

Oggie didn't get it, but everybody who knew Donnica could tell that the reason she was helping Oggie was in order to get something for herself. And it worked, too. Once the papers got wind that Oggie's manager was a pretty little ten-year-old girl, they went nuts taking pictures of Donnica and Oggie together. *HT*, seeing the potential for even more publicity for the upcoming show, invited her to come with him to Hollywood. Donnica's ego immediately grew from large to jumbo size.

"Have you noticed she's calling people 'darling'?" Dawn said to Hannah one day at lunch.

"And now she's wearing sunglasses all the time, too," said Hannah. "The whole thing makes me sick."

Amy just shook her head.

Pretty soon, the papers started running stories about which contestants would prove to be the biggest competition for Oggie.

"You think Oggie can beat that guy with the stretchy nostrils?" Bethie Hudson asked one day.

"Of course he can beat him," said Donnica. "What's so great about being able to put quarters up your nose?"

"What about the girl who paints with pudding?" asked someone else.

"Who cares about pudding?" Donnica said, although truthfully the girl's remarkably accurate version of the *Mona Lisa* made entirely out of chocolate pudding had made her a little bit nervous.

"I've been thinking, maybe charving states isn't good enough," Donnica told Oggie one day at lunch. "What about presidents? You could charve Abe Lincoln with his top hat on. Or George Washington chopping down the cherry tree."

"That sounds kind of complicated," said Oggie.

"You want to win, don't you?" barked Donnica, pulling out her stopwatch. "Come on, Oggie Cooder. Give me George Washington and the cherry tree — and make it good!"

Oggie sighed and pulled a fresh piece of cheese out of his pocket. Charving sure was a lot less fun than it used to be.

On Friday, two days before Oggie and Donnica were supposed to fly to California to tape the show, Mr. Snolinovsky asked to see Oggie out in the hall.

"I'd better come, too," said Donnica. "I don't like my client to be interviewed when I'm not present."

"Donnica," Mr. Snolinovksy told her firmly, "go back to your seat, please. During school hours

Oggie is not your client, he is my student. And please don't make me say this again: *No sunglasses in my classroom.*"

Out in the hall, Mr. Snolinovsky leaned against the wall and scratched his head.

"Is there anything you'd like to talk about, Oggie?" he asked.

Oggie thought for a second. "Well," he said, "I have always kind of wondered why you scratch your head so much. When Turk is itchy, it usually means it's time for a flea bath."

Mr. Snolinovsky looked flustered. "I meant about the show," he said. "Are you sure it's not too much, all of this Hollywood hoo-ha?"

Oggie laughed. He liked that word "hoo-ha."

"I'm okay," he said. "My stomach feels kind of weird sometimes, though. I think it might be my appendix."

"It's more likely that you're nervous."

"The funny thing is," said Oggie, "I used to charve when I felt nervous. But ever since Donnica started timing me, and making me charve George Washington, it's not so relaxing anymore."

"Donnica can be a very persuasive girl," said Mr. Snolinovsky.

"Does persuasive mean the same thing as really bossy?" asked Oggie.

Mr. Snolinovsky laughed. "Just remember to be yourself, Oggie, and I'm sure you'll be fine."

At the end of the day, Mr. Snolinovsky dragged out his record player and the desks got pushed to the side of the room for square dancing. The first dance was a "ladies' choice" and all the girls made a beeline for Oggie. Everybody wanted to dance with the most famous fourth grader in Wawatosa, Wisconsin. That is, *almost* everybody. Amy stood in the corner watching Oggie and quietly shaking her head.

When Oggie and Donnica got home from school, Bradley Mathis's car was parked in the Cooders' driveway again. Mr. and Mrs. Cooder were down at the store, meeting with another plumber, so no one had been home to answer the doorbell, leaving Brad no choice but to wait on the porch steps.

"Oggie, we've got a problem," he said.

"Sorry, Brad, but before I do anything else I have to take Turk out," Oggie apologized. "Otherwise I might end up with the kind of problem that leaves a stain on the rug."

While Oggie walked Turk, Donnica sat down next to Brad on the steps and asked him what was the matter.

"The problem is, Oggie Fever is spreading faster than we thought it would. It's gone way beyond Wawatosa. Kids all over the country are starting to dress like him and act like him. They're saying 'yeppers.' And adopting shaggy dogs from the pound, crocheting shoelaces, and charving cheese. He's even got a fan club with a Web site — Prrrrip.com."

"Isn't that a good thing?" asked Donnica, who would have given anything to have a fan club.

"You would think so," said Brad. "But the show won't air for another month after the taping, and the producers are worried that Oggie Cooder will be old news by that time. People won't care anymore."

Donnica felt her free ride to Hollywood slipping through her fingers.

"There has to be something we can do," she said, quickly jumping up. She pulled her lip gloss out of her pocket and began pacing nervously as she ran it over her lips. Suddenly, she stopped.

"I've got it!" Donnica said excitedly. "It's the exact same thing as the toaster! We have to turn up the dial!"

Brad looked confused. "On the toaster?" he asked.

"No, on Oggie. We have to turn up the dial on Oggie and make him *Oggier*," Donnica said.

A smile slowly spread across Brad's face.

"You know what?" he said. "I think you might be onto something here. Make Oggie *Oggier*, huh? I like it!"

19

In the time that it took Oggie to walk Turk around the block, Donnica and Brad had come up with a plan for how to make Oggie *Oggier*. Brad made several phone calls, then drove off in a hurry. Two minutes later, Donnica took off on her bicycle in the opposite direction.

"Where is everybody?" Oggie wondered aloud when he and Turk got back.

Thump! Thump! Thump!

Oggie heard a strange sound outside.

"Hey, Oggie!" someone called.

Oggie ran to the window and looked out. David Korben was standing in the driveway bouncing his basketball.

Thump! Thump! Thump!

"Hi, David," said Oggie as he came outside and stood on the porch. "What's up?"

"I just saw old bossy face ride off on her bicycle, so I figured maybe this would be a good time to come over and see if you want to play some B-ball."

"You mean now?" asked Oggie. "With you?"

"Sure, why not?" David said.

"I can't. I have to practice my charving. Donnica says my Ulysses S. Grant looks too much like Santa Claus."

"Oh, come on," said David. "The guys are all over at the courts by the school, waiting. We really want you to play with us."

"But Donnica says —"

"Who cares what she says?" interrupted David. "You can't spend all your time charving, can you? Besides, if you hang around with cheese too much, you might turn into a mouse, or something."

Oggie laughed.

"Well . . . maybe I could come play for a little while," he said.

His whole life Oggie had always been the last one picked when teams were being chosen for sports. But that day on the basketball court, David Korben won the coin toss, which meant he got first pick. He didn't even hesitate —

"I want Oggie."

Oggie grinned so hard his face hurt. And during the game, when he dribbled the ball out of bounds, or missed a basket, instead of laughing at him and calling him names, the boys gave him pointers.

"Step into it when you pass!"

"Bend your knees before you shoot!"

"Take your time, Cooder."

Oggie listened to everything they said, and he concentrated on playing basketball just the way he concentrated when he was charving cheese. Finally, it paid off and he made a basket! In fact, he made three.

"That was really fun," Oggie told the guys as they took turns at the drinking fountain after the game. "Thanks for helping me."

"No problem," said David, wiping his mouth with the back of his hand. "It's not every day we get to play with somebody famous like you."

Oggie blushed and grinned. Maybe this whole celebrity thing wasn't so bad. After all, he'd never been invited to play basketball before.

"Hey, Oggie," said one of the guys, "since you're the pro, how about you give us some charving lessons?"

"Sure," said Oggie.

"OVER MY DEAD BODY!"

Nobody had noticed Donnica's arrival. She'd been riding by the school on her way home and had noticed Oggie on the basketball court. She was furious.

"How dare you!" she shouted.

"What's the big deal, Donnica?" said David, "He was just playing a little B-ball. And you know something? He's not half bad."

Oggie started to *prrrrr-ip* from the compliment, but the look on Donnica's face stopped him cold.

"We're going," Donnica said, grabbing Oggie's arm and pulling him off the court. "Brad is probably already there waiting with the new cheese."

Oggie reluctantly waved good-bye to the guys. Donnica got back on her bike and told Oggie to run along beside her.

"How come Brad went to get more cheese?" Oggie asked, doing his best to keep up with Donnica. "I told you, my mom bought a whole bunch yesterday."

"That cheese is no good anymore," said Donnica. "We have to go bigger."

"Bigger?" said Oggie. He winced as his stomach pinched.

Donnica hit a bump in the road and put her hand out to steady the small cardboard box sitting in the basket attached to her handlebars.

"What's in there?" Oggie asked.

"That's for me to know and you to find out," Donnica answered mysteriously.

*   *   *

Brad was waiting on the steps when Oggie and Donnica arrived back at the Cooders' house.

"Did you get the cheese?" Donnica asked him.

Brad nodded.

"It's in the trunk. How about you? Did you find what you were looking for?"

Donnica carefully lifted the box out of her bike basket.

"It's perfect," she said. "Wait till you see."

Oggie opened the front door and let them in. Donnica carried the box inside and set it down on the floor. Oggie wasn't sure, but he thought he saw it move. Then he heard a strange whining sound. So did Turk, and the fur on the back of his neck stood up as he growled.

"What's in there?" Oggie asked again.

Donnica opened the box, reached in, and pulled out a small strange-looking creature with a pointy face like a rat and bumpy grayish-purple skin. The only fur on its body was a ratty pom-pom on the end of its tail and a tangle of white hair sprouting up from between its ears like a bad toupee.

"What *is* that?" gasped Oggie in horror.

"Oggie," said Donnica, scooping up the hideous creature and holding it out to him, "say hello to your new dog."

20

urk barked, and the strange little dog pulled back her lips and showed him her teeth.

"What kind of a dog is that?" Oggie asked. "And why doesn't it have any fur?"

"It's called a Chinese Crested. I got it at The Pet Stop. Her name is Fuzzy."

"That's a pretty strange name for a bald dog," Oggie said.

Donnica turned to Brad.

"Didn't I tell you she was perfect?" she said.

"Like Turk, only Turkier." Brad laughed.

"What's that supposed to mean?" asked Oggie.

But instead of answering, Brad hurried outside, returning a minute later with a big wooden box.

Oggie took one side of the heavy box and helped carry it into the living room where they put it down on the coffee table.

"Phew, that sure is heavy. What's in there?"

"Cheese," Brad told him.

"Cheese?" said Oggie. "But it weighs a ton."

"Seventy-five pounds," said Brad.

"*You bought seventy-five pounds of cheese?*" Oggie couldn't believe it.

"Actually, I bought one hundred and fifty pounds. There's another box just like this one out in the car."

"Why do we need so much?" Oggie asked.

"Do you want to explain?" Brad asked Donnica.

"It's like cheese . . . only cheesier," Donnica said.

Oggie groaned and flopped down on the couch.

"Can somebody *please* tell me what's going on?" he said.

So Donnica and Brad explained to Oggie the studio's concerns about people burning out on "Oggie Fever."

"You don't want to be old news, do you?" Donnica said.

But before Oggie could tell her that he wouldn't mind being old news if it meant he could take a break from all the speed-charving she'd been making him do — the doorbell rang.

"That must be LaRue," said Brad.

"Who's LaRue?" asked Oggie.

Brad opened the door, and a tall woman in a gold jumpsuit and a turban breezed into the house.

She was holding several large garment bags and a Styrofoam head with a curly red wig on it.

"Which one is Oogie?" she purred, looking around the room.

"Uh, actually it's *Oggie*," Oggie told her. "With two *g*'s, not two *o*'s."

"LaRue is a costume designer I happen to know in the area," Brad explained. "She's been kind enough to agree to help us with your new look."

"New look?" said Oggie, "I thought you said I looked okay the way I was."

"That was before, this is now," said Donnica.

Turk, who normally loved having company in the house, was lying under the coffee table nervously looking up at Fuzzy, who was sitting on a throw pillow on the couch licking herself.

"I must see this *chooving* thing before I can pick the outfit," said LaRue.

"Do you mean charving?" asked Oggie.

LaRue pulled a tape measure out of the pocket of her jumpsuit and began to measure Oggie.

"Hush, Oogie," she said, pressing a long finger up to her lips. "No worries. LaRue will find something yummy for you."

While LaRue measured, Brad opened the wooden box, revealing a giant chunk of cheddar cheese.

"How am I supposed to charve that?" asked Oggie. "It's not even sliced."

"I told you," said Donnica, "no more slices. We're going bigger."

"Much bigger," said Brad. "Are you ready for this? You're going to be charving Mount Rushmore!"

"*Mount Rushmore?*" cried Oggie.

"It'll be easy," said Donnica. "You already know how to do all those presidents, remember?"

"I'm ready to see the chooving now," said LaRue, putting her tape measure away. "Show me the chooving, Oggie."

Oggie's head was spinning. Things were happening so fast.

"Ouch!" he exclaimed, as his stomach pinched sharply.

"Come on," said Donnica, pulling out her stop-watch, "we don't have much time left. You have to practice."

"I don't even remember what Mount Rushmore looks like!" Oggie protested.

"Don't worry," Brad told him, "I picked up a book about famous American landmarks. There's a picture of Mount Rushmore on page thirty-three."

"I don't know about this," said Oggie uncertainly, eyeing the huge piece of cheese sitting on the table in front of him.

"Trust me," said Donnica. Oggie's stomach pinched again.

As Oggie had suspected, *charving* Mount Rushmore turned out to be much more challenging than Donnica and Brad had made it out to be. For one thing, cheddar cheese had a different texture from American cheese. It was more apt to crumble, which was why Abraham Lincoln's nose and George Washington's eyebrows kept falling off.

Turk enjoyed gobbling up the scraps of cheese as they fell on the floor, but Oggie was miserable.

"Stop!" shouted LaRue, who had been perched on the arm of a chair nearby taking notes the whole time. "I see yellow!"

Oggie immediately looked at the rug to see if Turk had had an accident. But LaRue was talking about the clothes she wanted Oggie to wear.

"No more *chooving* now, Oogie. Time for LaRue to make you yummy."

Turk tried to join them as Oggie followed LaRue into the guest room. But LaRue pushed Turk away with her foot and closed the door in his face.

"I'm thinking knickers," LaRue said, unzipping one of her bags.

"Knickers?" said Oggie.

"Yummy yellow knickers," said LaRue.

Oggie had no idea what she was talking about.

"Can I still wear my shoelaces?" he asked. "They're pretty yummy, don't you think?"

LaRue looked at Oggie's feet and frowned.

"No," she said. "No, no no."

"What about striped pants?" asked Oggie. "Or maybe a checkered shirt? I'd be comfortable in those."

But Oggie's "new look" was not going to have stripes or checks. It was going to have yummy yellow knickers. As the final pieces of the let's-make-Oggie-Oggier plan fell into place, Oggie's stomach pinched harder and he wondered how much more he could take.

21

hile Oggie was busy getting his fashion makeover, Brad went out to the car to bring in the other box of cheese.

"Why are there so many reporters outside?" Brad asked, a few minutes later as he came in carrying the heavy box.

Donnica knew why they were there. Without telling anyone, she had called a press conference to stir up some excitement.

"I'll take care of them," she said, quickly pulling out her lip gloss and applying a fresh coat before heading outside to face the cameras.

Donnica loved dealing with the press. As they crowded around her with their cameras and notepads ready, she informed them that her "client" was involved in some top-secret last-minute preparations for the show and would not be available to speak with them. But they were more than welcome to take as many pictures of *her* as they wanted.

Back inside, LaRue and Brad were sitting on the couch with Fuzzy between them, waiting for Oggie to come out and model the outfit LaRue had chosen for him to wear on the show.

"What's taking so long, Oogie?" LaRue called impatiently. "Do you need help with the zippers?"

"No!" shouted Oggie, who had absolutely insisted that he did not want LaRue in the room with him while he was getting dressed. "I'll be out in a minute."

When Oggie finally did emerge, his face was so red it looked like he had a sunburn.

"I don't know about this outfit," Oggie said uncertainly. He peeked around the corner before shuffling uncomfortably out into the living room. He had on a pair of bright yellow pants that only came down to his knees, a shirt with giant buttons

and extremely puffy sleeves, and on his feet, a pair of wooden clogs like the kind Dutch people wear. The curly red wig was in his hand.

"Don't you have any pants that go all the way down?" he asked.

"Knickers are more yummy for you," said LaRue with a dismissive wave of her hand. "Put on the wig."

"It's itchy," Oggie complained.

Unconcerned with his discomfort, LaRue came over and put the wig on Oggie's head.

"It does kind of work, Oogie, I mean, Oggie," said Brad.

Oggie gasped as the worst stomach cramp so far hit him. He folded over in pain, and that's when he noticed the back door was ajar.

"Where's Turk?" he asked anxiously.

"The big dog?" LaRue responded. "With all the hair?"

"Yes," Oggie told her. "Where is the big dog?"

"He let it out," LaRue said with a little wave toward Brad.

"*What?*" cried Oggie.

"I turned my back for two seconds and he ate half of Mount Rushmore," Brad explained, "so I put him outside. I figured it was okay, since the yard is fenced in."

But what Brad didn't know was that the latch on the gate was broken. When Oggie ran out into the backyard, he found that the worst possible thing had happened.

Turk was gone!

22

ggie kicked off the heavy wooden shoes, jammed his feet into his sneakers, and took off.

"What are you doing?" Donnica screamed when Oggie burst out the door. "Don't let them see you! You'll ruin everything!"

The minute the reporters caught sight of Oggie, of course the cameras started clicking furiously. And they followed him as he ran up the street, whistling and frantically calling Turk's name.

Finally, Oggie caught sight of Turk, scratching under the big bush on the corner. He'd gone to retrieve the tennis ball he'd left there the other day.

"There you are," said Oggie, relieved. But when he reached out to grab hold of Turk's collar, the dog growled at him.

Oggie was stunned. Turk had never growled at him before. Ever. He only did that to strangers or people he didn't trust.

"What's the matter, Turkey?" cried Oggie in dismay. "Don't you like me anymore?"

Hot and sweaty from running, Oggie reached up to scratch his head and suddenly he understood. No wonder Turk had growled at him — he didn't recognize him!

"Okay, okay, I get the message, boy," Oggie said. He yanked off the red wig and threw it on the ground. Then he ripped off the ridiculous shirt, sending several of the big buttons flying. He would have taken off those silly yellow pants, too, except the photographers had caught up with him and he didn't want them taking pictures of him in his underwear. Brad was there by now, and so was LaRue, with the hideous Fuzzy under her arm. Turk, no longer confused, was barking and jumping up on Oggie to lick his face. But the happy reunion between boy and dog did not last long.

"Do you have any idea what you've done?" Donnica

shouted as she pushed her way through the crowd. "I told you not to let them see you. You've ruined all our hard work. What's the matter with you? Don't you want to go to Hollywood? Don't you want to be the most famous fourth grader in the world? What is your problem, Oggie Cooder? *DON'T YOU WANT TO WIN?*"

Oggie felt a monster stomach cramp beginning to rise up inside of him.

The crowd grew silent as they waited for him to respond. And in the quiet, Oggie finally found the answer to the question Donnica had asked him so many times.

"No, Donnica," he said, shaking his head. "I don't want to win. *You* do."

Donnica's eyes were ablaze.

"That's right," she snarled through gritted teeth. "And we made a deal, Oggie Cooder. I'm your manager, and I say that we are going to Hollywood together whether you like it or not. Now pick up your hair and get moving."

Oggie didn't move.

"I said, *PICK UP YOUR HAIR*," Donnica commanded, pointing at the red wig lying on the sidewalk.

Oggie took a deep breath.

"First of all," he said, "that is *not* my hair. And second of all, I don't want to charve Mount Rushmore. And third of all, that bald rat over there is not my dog. And fourth of all, these are definitely *not* my pants."

Oggie stopped to catch his breath.

"Are you finished?" snapped Donnica.

"Not quite," Oggie told her. And that's when Mr. Snolinovsky's words came back to him. Not the ones about how important it was to be yourself — he'd figured that part out when his own dog hadn't been able to recognize him. It was the other thing he'd said that Oggie felt was just right for this occasion. "Fifth of all," he said to Donnica, "I've had enough of this Hollywood hoo-ha."

As the reporters scribbled notes for their final Oggie Cooder stories, Turk barked happily, then grabbed his tennis ball.

For the first time in days, Oggie's stomach didn't ache. He actually felt happy, from the top of his head right down to the tips of his crocheted shoelaces.

"Come on, boy," Oggie said to Turk. "Let's go home."

23

After saying good-bye to *Hidden Talents*, Oggie Cooder's life went back to normal . . . even if it was a different kind of normal than before. Everybody in town knew who he was now, but nobody wanted to write newspaper articles about him anymore. Sales of American cheese slices leveled off, and kids went back to wearing regular shoelaces. David Korben and his buddies were shocked at first when they heard that Oggie had given up a chance to be on TV. But they decided it was pretty cool the way he'd stood up to Donnica Perfecto, and Oggie was invited to become a regular player at their after-school basketball games.

Dawn Perchy and Hannah Hummerman eventually forgave Donnica for what she'd done. They went back to eating lunch together at the table by the window, although Dawn and Hannah absolutely refused to finish her words for her anymore. And as for Donnica Perfecto, she held tight to her grudge against Oggie Cooder, vowing that someday she would get him back for ruining her plans to go to Hollywood. Especially when, in a rare showing of parental backbone, Mrs. Perfecto handed her daughter a spatula and insisted that she scrape the cheese off her ceiling.

Oggie was as happy as a clam. The only thing he regretted about deciding not to go on *Hidden Talents* was that he had planned to give the ten thousand dollars to his parents to pay for new pipes. The cost of the pipes became less of an issue, though, when a collector who'd read about the Cooders' store in one of the many newspaper articles written about Oggie stopped in and bought that old Howdy Doody hat for a very large sum of money.

Mr. Snolinovsky gave Oggie an A on his story about Turk and the licorice. He also wrote some very nice things about Oggie on his report card, including this: *"Oggie's positive attitude and his good self-esteem make him an excellent role model for his classmates."* Mrs. Cooder beamed proudly as she glued the report card into the family scrapbook.

One Friday afternoon, Mr. Snolinovsky's fourth graders pushed their desks to the side of the room and got ready to square-dance. The first dance was a "ladies choice," and Amy Schneider chose Oggie to be her partner.

"So, are you coming over, Oggie?" she asked as they hooked elbows and began to swing each other around. "My mom said she would make us popcorn and root beer floats if we want."

The final episode of *Hidden Talents* was going to be on that night, and since Amy knew that Oggie didn't have a TV at home, she had invited him to come over and watch it at her house.

"What time did you say it starts?" asked Oggie.

Amy was about to answer when Oggie tripped on one of his shoelaces and accidentally stepped on her foot.

"Ouch!" cried Amy, but then she giggled and told him to be there at eight o' clock.

The girl who painted with pudding ended up winning the grand prize on *Hidden Talents* that night. As Oggie sat on Amy Schneider's couch happily munching popcorn and watching the television audience go nuts, clapping and cheering, he couldn't contain himself, either.

"*Prrrrr-ip! Prrrrr-ip!*" went Oggie. Because even though it wasn't him up there on that Hollywood stage, Oggie Cooder finally knew what it felt like to be a winner, and he thought it was just about the best feeling in the world.